Anno Domini 2000; Or, Woman's Destiny

Anno Domini 2000; Or, Woman's Destiny

Sir Julius Vogel

MINT EDITIONS

Anno Domini 2000; Or, Woman's Destiny was first published in 1889.

This edition published by Mint Editions 2021.

ISBN 9781513215464 | E-ISBN 9781513213460

Published by Mint Editions®

 MINT
EDITIONS

minteditionbooks.com

Publishing Director: Jennifer Newens
Design & Production: Rachel Lopez Metzger
Project Manager: Micaela Clark
Typesetting: Westchester Publishing Services

Contents

Prologue

George Claude Sonsius in his early youth appeared to have before him a fair, prosperous future. His father and mother were of good family, but neither of them inherited wealth. When young Sonsius finished his university career, the small fortune which his father possessed was swept away by the failure of a large banking company. All that remained from the wreck was a trifling annuity payable during the lives of his father and mother, and this they did not live long to enjoy. They died within a year of each other, but they had been able to obtain for their son a fairly good position in a large mercantile house as foreign correspondent. At twenty-five the young man married; and three years afterwards he unfortunately met with a serious accident, that made him for two years a helpless invalid and at the end of the time left him with his right hand incapable of use. Meanwhile his appointment had lapsed, his wife's small fortune had disappeared, and during several years his existence had been one continual struggle with ever-increasing want and penury. The end was approaching. The father and mother and their one crippled son, twelve years old, dwelt in the miserable attic of a most dilapidated house in one of the poorest neighbourhoods of London. The roof over their heads did not even protect them from the weather. The room was denuded of every article of furniture with the exception of two worthless wooden cases and a horsehair mattress on which the unhappy boy stretched his pain-wrung limbs.

Early in life this child suffered only from weakness of the spine, but his parents could afford no prolonged remedial measures. Not that they were unkind to him. On the contrary, they devoted to him every minute they could spare, and lavished on him all the attention that affection comparatively powerless from want of means could dictate. But the food they were able to give him was scant instead of, as his condition demanded, varied and nutritious. At length chronic disease of the spine set in, and his life became one long misery.

Parochial aid was refused unless they would go into the poor-house, but the one thing Mrs. Sonsius could not bring herself to endure was the separation from her son which was demanded of her as a condition of relief.

For thirty hours they had been without food, when the father, maddened by the moanings of his wife and child, rushed into the street, and passing a baker's shop which appeared to be empty, stole from it a loaf of bread. The proprietor, however, saw the action from an inner room. He caught Sonsius just as he was leaving the shop. He did not care to give the thief in charge, necessitating as it would several attendances at the police court. He took the administration of justice into his own hands, and dealt the unhappy man two severe blows in the face. To a healthy person the punishment would have done comparatively little harm, but Sonsius was weakened by disease and starvation, and the shock of the blows was too much for him. He fell prone on the pavement, and all attempts to restore him to consciousness proved unavailing.

Then his history became public property. Scores of people remembered the pleasant-mannered, well-looking young man who had distinguished himself at college, and for whom life seemed to promise a pleasant journey. The horrible condition of his wife and child, the desperation that drove him to the one lapse from an otherwise stainless life, the frightful contrast between the hidden poverty and the gorgeous wealth of the great metropolis, became themes upon which every newspaper dilated after its own fashion. Some papers even went so far as to ask, "Was it a crime for a man to steal a loaf of bread to save his wife and child from starvation?"

In grim contrast with the terrible conclusion of his wretched career, the publicity cast upon it elicited the fact that a few weeks earlier he had inherited by the death of a distant relative an enormous fortune, all efforts to trace him through the changes of residence that increasing poverty had necessitated having proved unavailing. Now that the wretched father and husband was dead, the wife for whom the bread was stolen had become a great lady, the boy was at length to receive the aid that wealth could give him. Poor George Claude Sonsius has nothing to do with our story, but his fate led to the alleviation of a great deal of misery that otherwise might have been in store for millions of human beings.

Loud and clear rang out the cry, "What was the use of denouncing slavery when want like this was allowed to pass unheeded by the side of superfluous wealth?" The slave-owner has sufficient interest in his slaves, it was alleged, as a rule, to care for their well-being. Even criminals were clothed and fed.

Had not, it was asked, every human being the right to demand from a world which through the resources of experience and science became constantly more productive a sufficiency of sustenance?

The inquest room was crowded. The coroner and jury were strongly affected as they viewed the body laid out in a luxuriously appointed coffin. Wealth denied to the living was lavished on the dead. No longer in rags and tatters, the lifeless body seemed to revert to the past. Shrunken as was the frame, and emaciated the features, there remained evidence sufficient to show that the now inanimate form was once a fine and handsome man.

The evidence was short, and the summing up of the coroner decisive. He insisted that the baker had not wilfully committed wrong and should not be made responsible for the consequences that followed his rough recovery of his property. A butcher and a general provision dealer on the jury took strongly the same view. How were poor tradesmen to protect themselves? They must take the law in their own hands, they argued, otherwise it would be better to submit to being robbed rather than waste their time in police courts. They wanted a verdict of justifiable homicide. Another juryman (a small builder) urged a verdict of misadventure; at first he called it peradventure. But the rest of the jury felt otherwise. Some desired a verdict of manslaughter, and it was long before the compromise of "Death by accident" was agreed to.

Deep groans filled the room as the result was announced. That same night a large crowd of men and women assembled outside the baker's shop with hostile demonstrations. The windows were destroyed, and an attempt made to break in the door. A serious riot would probably have ensued but for the arrival of a large body of police.

Again the fate of George Sonsius became the familiar topic of the press. But the impression was not an ephemeral one.

The fierce spirit of discontent which for years had been smouldering burst into flames. A secret society called the "Live and Let Live" was formed, with ramifications throughout the world. The force of numbers, the force of brute strength, was appealed to.

A bold and outspoken declaration was made that every human being had an inherent right to sufficient food and clothing and comfortable lodging. Truly poor George Sonsius died for the good of many millions of his fellow-creatures. Our history will show the point at length achieved.

Shortly after poor Sonsius' death a remarkable meeting was held in the city of London. The representatives of six of the largest financial houses throughout the globe assembled by agreement to discuss the present material condition of the world and its future prospects. There was Lord de Cardrosse, head of the English house of that name and chief, moreover, of the family, whose branches presided over princely houses of finance in six of the chief cities of the continent of Europe. Second only in power in Great Britain, the house of Bisdat and Co. was represented by Charles James Bisdat, a man of scarcely forty, but held to be the greatest living authority on abstruse financial questions. The Dutch house of Von Serge Brothers was represented by its head, Cornelius Julius Von Serge. The greatest finance house in America, Rorgon, Bryce and Co., appeared by its chief, Henry Tudor Rorgon; and the scarcely less powerful house of Lockay, Stanfield and Co., of San Francisco, Melbourne, Sydney, and Wellington, was represented by its chief, Alfred Demetrius. The German and African house of Werther, Scribe and Co. was present in the person of its head, Baron Scribe; and the French and Continental houses of the De Cardrosse family were represented by the future head of the family, the Baroness de Cardrosse. The deliberations were carried on in French.

Two or more of these houses had no doubt from time to time worked together in one transaction; but their uniform position was one of independence towards each other, verging more towards antagonism than to union. In fact, the junction for ordinary purposes of such vast powers as these kings of finance wielded would be fatal to liberty and freedom.

A single instance will suffice to show the power referred to, which even one group of financiers could wield.

Five years previously all Europe was in a ferment. War was expected from every quarter. It depended not on one, but on many questions. The alliances were doubtful. Nothing seemed certain but that neutrality would be impossible, and that the Continent would be divided into two or more great camps. The final decision appeared to rest with Great Britain. There an ominous disposition for war was displaying itself. The inclination of the Sovereign and the Cabinet was supposed to be in that direction. But the family of De Cardrosses throughout Europe was for peace. The chief of the family was the head of the English house, and it was decided he should interview the Prime Minister of England and acquaint him with the views of this great financial group. His reception was not flattering; but if he felt mortified, he did not show it. He expressed himself deeply sensible of the honour done to him by his being allowed to state his opinions; and with a reverential inclination he bowed himself from the presence of the greatest statesman of his day, the Right Honourable Randolph Stanley. That afternoon it was bruited about that, in view of coming possibilities, the De Cardrosse family had determined to realise securities all over Europe and send gold to America. The next morning a disposition to sell was reported from every direction, and five millions sterling of gold were collected for despatch to New York. In twenty-four hours there was a panic throughout Great Britain and Europe. The Bank of England asked for permission to suspend specie payments, but could indicate no limit to which such a permission should be set. It seemed as if Europe would be drained of gold.

The great rivals of the De Cardrosses looked on and either could not or would not interfere. A hurried Cabinet meeting was convened, and as a result a conference by telephone was arranged between the Prime Minister of Great Britain and the Ministers of the Great Powers of Europe. Commencing by twos and threes, the conference developed into an assemblage for conversational purposes of at least twenty of the chief statesmen and diplomatists of the Old World. Rumour said that even monarchs in two or three cases were present and inspired the telephonic utterances of their Ministers. How the result was arrived at was known best to those who took part in the conference, but peace and disarmament were agreed on if certain contingencies involving the exercise of vast power and the expenditure of enormous capital could be provided for. No other conclusion could be arrived at, and one way or the other the outcome had to be settled within twenty-four hours. The conference had lasted from ten o'clock to four. At five o'clock by invitation Lord de Cardrosse waited on the Prime Minister, who received him much more cordially than before.

"You have caused me," he said, "to learn a great deal during the last forty-eight hours."

"I could not presume to teach you anything. Events have spoken," was the reply.

"And who controlled them if not the houses of De Cardrosse?"

"You do us too much honour. It is you who govern; we are of those who are governed."

"The alliance between power and modesty," said the Prime Minister, with pardonable irony, "is irresistible. Tell me, my Lord, is it too late for your views to prevail?"

A slight, almost imperceptible start was the only movement the De Cardrosse made. The enormous self-repression he was exercising cannot be exaggerated. The future strength of the family depended on the issue. There was, however, no tremor in his voice when he answered, "If you adopt them, I do not think it is too late."

"But do you realise the sacrifices in all directions that have to be made?" said the Minister in faltering tones.

"I think I do."

"And you think to secure peace those sacrifices should be made?"

"I do."

"Will you tell me what those sacrifices are?" he asked.

Lord de Cardrosse smiled. "You desire me," he said, "to tell you what you already know." Then he proceeded to describe to the amazed Prime Minister in brief but pregnant terms one after the other the conditions that had been agreed on. Once only he paused and indicated that the condition he was describing he accepted reluctantly.

"I do not conceal," said the astounded Prime Minister, "my surprise at the extent of your knowledge; and clearly you approve the only compromise possible. It is needless to tell you that the acceptance of this compromise requires the use of means not at the disposal of the Governments. In one word, will it suit you to supply them?"

"I might," responded Lord de Cardrosse, "ask you until two o'clock tomorrow to give an answer; but I do not wish to add to your anxiety. If you will undertake to entirely and absolutely confine within your own breast the knowledge of what my answer will be, I will undertake that that answer at two o'clock tomorrow shall be 'Yes.'"

Silently they shook hands. Probably these two men had never before so thoroughly appreciated the strength and speciality of their several powers.

The panic continued until two o'clock the following day, when an enormous reaction took place. The part the De Cardrosse family played in securing peace was suspected by a few only. Its full extent the Prime Minister alone knew. He it was who enjoyed the credit for saving the world from a desolating war.

And now, after an interval of five years, the sovereigns of finance met in conclave. In obedience to the generally expressed wish, Lord de Cardrosse took the chair. "I need scarcely say," he began, "that I am deeply sensible of the compliment you pay me in asking me to preside over such a meeting. We in this room represent a living power throughout the globe, before which the reigning sovereigns of the world are comparatively helpless. But, because of our great strength, it is undesirable that we should work unitedly except for very great and humane objects. For the mere purpose of money-making, I feel assured you all agree with me in desiring no combination, no monopoly, that would pit us against the rest of the world."

He paused for a moment, evidently desiring to disguise the strength of the emotion with which he spoke.

He resumed in slower and apparently more mastered words. "I wish I could put it to you sufficiently strongly that our houses would not have considered any good that could result to them and to you a sufficient excuse for inviting such a combination. We hold that the only cause that could justify it is the conviction that for the good of mankind a vast power requires to be wielded which is not to be found in the ordinary machinery of government."

A murmur of applause went round the table; and Mr. Demetrius, with much feeling, said, "You make me very happy by the assurance you have given. I will not conceal from you that our house anticipated as much, or it would not have been represented. We are too largely concerned with States in which free institutions are permanent not to avoid anything which might savour of a disposition to combine financial forces for the benefit of financial houses."

Lord de Cardrosse then proceeded to explain that his family, in serious and prolonged conclave, could come to no other conclusion than that certain influences were at work which would cause great suffering to mankind and sap and destroy the best institutions which civilisation and science had combined to create. The time had come to answer the question, should human knowledge, human wants, and human skill continue to advance to an extent to which no limit could be put, or should the survival of the fittest and strongest be fought out in a period of anarchy?

"It amounts," he said in a tone of profound conviction, "to this: the ills under which the masses suffer accumulate. There is no use in comparing what they have today with what they had fifty years ago. A person who grows from infancy to manhood in a prison may feel contented until he knows what the liberty is that others enjoy. The born blind are happier than those who become blind by accident. To our masses the knowledge of liberty is open, and they feel they are needlessly deprived of it. Wider and wider to their increasing knowledge opens out the horizon of possible delights; more and more do they feel that they are deprived of what of right belongs to them."

He paused, as if inviting some remarks from his hearers.

Mr. Bisdat, who spoke in an interrogative rather than an affirmative tone, took up the thread.

"I am right, I think, in concluding that your remarks do not point against or in favour of any school of politics or doctrines of party. You direct our notice to causes below the surface to which the Government of the day—I had almost said the hour,—do not penetrate, causes which you believe, if left to unchecked operation, will undermine the whole social fabric."

"It is so," emphatically replied Lord de Cardrosse. "The evils are not only apparent; but equally apparent is it that no remedy is being applied, and that we are riding headlong to anarchy."

Again he paused, and Mr. Rorgon took up the discussion. "If we," he said, "the princes of finance, do not find a remedy, how long will the enlarged intelligence of the people submit to conditions which are at war with the theory of the equality and liberty of mankind?"

"Yes," said the Baroness de Cardrosse, speaking for the first time, "it is clear that there is a limit to the inequality of fortune to which men and women will submit. Equality of possessions there cannot be; but, if I may indulge in metaphor, we cannot expect that the bulk of humankind will be content with being entirely shut out from the sunlight of existence."

The gentlemen present bowed low in approval; and Mr. Demetrius said, "The simile of the Baroness is singularly appropriate. There are myriads of human beings to whom the sunshine of life is denied. A too universal evil invites resistance by means which in lesser cases might be scouted. In short, if the remedy is left to anarchy, anarchy there will be. Even in our young lands the shadow of the coming evil is beginning to show itself. Indeed," he added, with an air of musing abstraction, "it is not unfair to deduce from what has been said, that, even if the evils are less in the new lands of the West and the South, superior general intelligence may more than proportionally increase the wants of the multitude and the sense of wrong under which they labour."

The conference extended over three days. Everyone agreed that interference with the ordinary conditions of finance was inexpedient except in extreme cases, but they were unanimous in thinking that an extreme case had to be dealt with. They finally decided by the use of an extended paper currency, with its necessary guarantees, to increase the circulating medium and to raise the prices both of products and labour. Someother decisions were adopted having especial reference to the employment of labour and insurance against want in cases of disablement through illness, accident, or old age.

So ended the most remarkable conference of any age or time.

I

The Year 2000—United Britain

Time has passed. There have been many alterations, few of an extreme character. The changes are mostly the results of gradual developments worked out by the natural progress of natural laws. But as constant dropping wears away a stone, constant progression, comparatively imperceptible in its course, attains to immense distances after the lapse of time. This applies though the momentum continually increases the rate of the progress. Thus the well-being of the human kind has undoubtedly increased much more largely during the period between 1900 and 2000 than during the previous century, but equally in either century would it be difficult to select any five years as an example of the turning-point of advancement. Progression, progression, always progression, has been the history of the centuries since the birth of Christ. Doubtless the century we have now entered on will be yet more fruitful of human advancement than any of its predecessors. The strongest point of the century which

> *"Has gone, with its thorns and its roses,*
> *With the dust of dead ages to mix,"*

has been the astonishing improvement of the condition of mankind and the no less striking advancement of the intellectual power of woman.

The barriers which man in his own interest set to the occupation of woman having once been broken down, the progress of woman in all pursuits requiring judgment and intellect has been continuous; and the sum of that progress is enormous. It has, in fact, come to be accepted that the bodily power is greater in man, and the mental power larger in woman. So to speak, woman has become the guiding, man the executive, force of the world. Progress has necessarily become greater because it is found that women bring to the aid of more subtle intellectual capabilities faculties of imagination that are the necessary adjuncts of improvement. The arts and caprices which in old days were called feminine proved to be the silken chains fastened by men on women to lull them into inaction. Without abating any of their charms, women have long ceased to submit to be the playthings of men. They lead men, as of yore, but not so much through the fancy or the senses as through the legitimate consciousness of the man that in following woman's guidance he is tending to higher purposes. We are generalising of course to a certain extent. The variable extent of women's influence is now, as it has been throughout the ages past, the point on which most of the dramas of the human race depend.

The increased enjoyment of mankind is a no less striking feature of the last hundred years. Long since a general recognition was given to the theory that, whilst equality of possession was an impossible and indeed undesirable ideal, there should be a minimum of enjoyment of which no human being should be deprived unless on account of crime. Crime as an occupation has become unknown, and hereditary crime rendered impossible. On the other hand, the law has constituted such provisions for reserves of wealth that anything more than temporary destitution is precluded. Such temporary destitution can only be the result of sheer improvidence, the expenditure, for instance, within a day of what should be expended in a week. The moment it becomes evident, its recurrence is rendered impossible, because the assistance, instead of being given weekly, is rendered daily. Private charity has been minimised; indeed, it is considered to be injurious: and all laws for the recovery of debts have been abolished. The decision as to whether there is debt and its amount is still to be obtained, but the satisfaction of all debt depends solely on the sense of honour or expediency of the debtor. The posting the name of a debtor who refuses to satisfy his liabilities has been found to be far more efficacious than any process of law.

The enjoyment of what in the past would have been considered luxuries has become general. The poorest household has with respect to comforts and provisions a profusion which a hundred years since was wanting in households of the advanced classes.

Long since there dawned upon the world the conviction—

First. That labour or work of some kind was the only condition of general happiness.

Second. That every human being was entitled to a certain proportion of the world's good things.

Third. That, as the capacity of machinery and the population of the world increased production, the theory of the need of labour could not be realised unless with a corresponding increase of the wants of mankind; and that, instead of encouraging a degraded style of living, it was in the interests of the happiness of mankind to encourage a style of living in which the refinements of life received marked consideration.

Great Britain, as it used to be called, has long ceased to be a bundle of sticks. The British dominions have been consolidated into the empire of United Britain; and not only is it the most powerful empire on the globe, but at present no sign is shown of any tendency to weakness or decay. Yet there was a time—about the year 1920—when the utter disintegration of the Empire seemed not only possible, but probable.

The Irish question was still undecided. For many years it had continued to be the sport of Ministers. Cabinet succeeded Cabinet; each had its Irish nostrum; each seemed to think that the Irish question was a good means of delaying questions nearer home. The power of the nation sensibly waned. What nation could be strong with pronounced disaffection festering in its midst? At length, when rumours of a great war were rife upon the result of which the very existence of Great Britain as a nation might depend, the Colonies interposed. By this time the Canadian, Australasian, and Cape colonies had become rich, populous, and powerful. United, they far exceeded in importance the original mother-country.

At the instigation of the Premier of Canada, a confidential intercolonial conference was held. In consequence of the deliberations that ensued, a united representation was made to the Prime Minister of England to the effect that the Colonies could no longer regard without concern the prolonged disquiet prevailing in Ireland. They would suffer should any disaster overtake the Empire, and disaster was courted by permitting the continuation of Irish disaffection. Besides, the Colonies, enjoying as they did local government, could see no reason why Ireland should be treated differently. The message was a mandate, and was meant to be so. The Prime Minister of England, however, puffed up with the pride of old traditions, did not or would not so understand it, and returned an insolent answer. Within twenty-four hours the Colonial Ministers sent a joint respectful address to the King of England representing that they were equally his Majesty's advisers with his Ministers residing in England, and refusing to make any further communications to or through his present advisers.

The Ministry had to retire; a new one was formed. Ireland received the boon it had long claimed of local government, and the whole Empire was federated on the condition that the federation was irrevocable and that every part of it should fight to the last to preserve the union. The King of England and Emperor of India was crowned amidst great pomp Emperor of Britain. All parts of the Empire joined their strength and resources. A federal fleet was formed on the basis that it was to equal in power in every respect the united fleets of all the rest of the world. Conferences with the Great Powers took place in consequence of which Egypt, Belgium, and the whole of the ports bordering the English Channel and Straits of Dover, and the whole of South Africa became incorporated into the empire of Britain. Some concessions, however, were made in other directions. These results were achieved within fifteen years of the interference by the Colonies in federal affairs, and the foundation was laid for the powerful empire which Britain has become. Two other empires and one republic alone approach it in power, and a cordial understanding exists between them to repress war to the utmost extent possible. They constitute the police of the world. Each portion of the Emperor of Britain's possessions enjoys local government, but the federal government is irresistibly strong. It is difficult to say which is the seat of government, as the Federal Parliament is held in different parts of the world, and the Emperor resides in many places. With the utmost comfort he can go from end to end of his dominions in twelve days.

If a headquarter does remain, it may probably be conceded that Alexandria fulfils that position.

The House of Lords has ceased to exist as a separate chamber. The peers began to feel ashamed of holding positions not in virtue of their abilities, but because of the accident of birth. It was they who first sought and ultimately obtained the right to hold seats in the elective branch of the Legislature; and finally it was decided that the peerage should elect a certain number of its own members to represent it in the Federal Parliament: in other words, the accidents of birth were controlled by the selection of the fittest.

Our scene opens in Melbourne, in the year 2000—a few years prior to the date at which we are writing. The Federal Parliament was sitting there that year. The Emperor occupied his magnificent palace on the banks of the Yarra, above Melbourne, which city and its suburbs possessed a population of nearly two millions.

In a large and handsome room in the Federal buildings, a young woman of about twenty-three years of age was seated. She was born in New Zealand. She entered the local parliament before she was twenty.[*] At twenty-two she was elected to the Federal Parliament, and she had now become Under-Secretary of State for Home Affairs. From her earliest youth she had never failed in any intellectual exercise. Her intelligence was considered phenomenal. Her name was Hilda Richmond Fitzherbert. She was descended from families which for upwards of a century produced distinguished statesmen—a word, it should be mentioned, which includes both sexes. She was fair to look at in both face and figure. Dark violet eyes, brown hair flecked with a golden tinge, clearly cut features, and a glorious complexion made up a face artistically perfect; but these charms were what the observer least noticed. The expression of the face was by far its chief attraction, and words fail to do justice to it. There was about it a luminous intelligence, a purity, and a pathos that seemed to belong to another world. No trace of passion yet stamped it. If the love given to all humanity ever became a love devoted to one person, the expression of the features might descend from the spiritual to the passionate. Even then to human gaze it might become more fascinating. But that test had not come. As she rose from her chair you saw that she was well formed, though slight in figure and of full height. She went to an instrument at a side-table, and spoke to it, the materials for some half-dozen letters referring to groups of papers that lay on the table. When she concluded, she summoned a secretary, who removed the papers and the phonogram on which her voice had been impressed. These letters were reproduced, and brought to her for signature. Copies attached to the several papers were initialled. Meanwhile she paced up and down the room in evident deep distraction. At length she summoned a messenger, and asked him to tell the Countess of Middlesex that she wished to see her. In a few minutes Lady Middlesex entered the room. She was about thirty years of age, of middle height, and pleasing appearance, though a close observer might imagine he saw something sinister in the expression of her countenance. After a somewhat ceremonious greeting, Miss Fitzherbert commenced: "I have carefully considered what passed at our last interview. It is difficult to separate our official and unofficial relations. I am still at a loss to determine whether you have spoken to me as the Assistant Under-Secretary to the Under-Secretary or as woman to woman."

---

[*] Every adult of eighteen years of age was allowed to vote and was consequently, by the laws of the Empire, eligible for election.

Lady Middlesex quickly rejoined, "Will you let me speak to you as woman to woman, and forget for a moment our official relations?"

"Can you doubt it?" replied Miss Fitzherbert. "But remember that our wishes are not always under our control, and that, though I may not desire to remember to your prejudice what you say, I may not be able to free myself from recollection."

"And yet," said Lady Middlesex, with scarcely veiled irony, "the world says Miss Fitzherbert does not know what prejudice means!"

The slightest possible movement of impatience was all the rejoinder vouchsafed to this speech.

Lady Middlesex continued, "I spoke to you as strongly as I dared, as strongly as my position permitted, about my brother Reginald—Lord Reginald Paramatta. He suffers under a sense of injury. He is miserable. He feels that it is to you that he owes his removal to a distant station. He loves you, and does not know if he may venture to tell you so."

"No woman," replied Miss Fitzherbert, "is warranted in regarding with anger the love of a good man; but you know, or ought to know, that my life is consecrated to objects that are inconsistent with my entertaining the love you speak of."

"But," said Lady Middlesex, "can you be sure that it always will be so?"

"We can be sure of nothing."

"Nay," replied Lady Middlesex, "do not generalise. Let me at least enjoy the liberty you have accorded me. If you did not feel that there were possibilities for Reginald in conflict with your indifference, why should you trouble yourself with his removal?"

"I have not admitted that I am concerned in his removal."

"You know you are; you cannot deny it."

Miss Fitzherbert was dismayed at the position into which she had allowed herself to be forced. She must either state what truth forbade or admit that to some extent Lord Reginald had obtained a hold on her thoughts.

"Other men," pursued Lady Middlesex, with remorseless directness, "have aspired as Reginald does; and you have known how to dispose of their aspirations without such a course as that of which my brother has been the object."

"I have understood," said Miss Fitzherbert, "that Lord Reginald is promoted to an important position, one that ought to be intensely gratifying to so comparatively young a man."

"My brother has only one wish, and you are its centre. He desires only one position."

"I did not infer, Lady Middlesex," said Miss Fitzherbert, with some haughtiness, "that you designed to use the permission you asked of me to become a suitor on your brother's behalf."

"Why else should I have asked such permission?" replied Lady Middlesex, with equal haughtiness. Then, with a sudden change of mood and manner, "Miss Fitzherbert, forgive me. My brother is all in all to me. My husband and my only child are dead. My brother is all that is left to me to remind me of a once happy home. Do not, I pray, I entreat you, embitter his life. Ask yourself—forgive me for saying so—if ambition rather than consecration to a special career may not influence you; and if your conscience replies affirmatively, remember the time will come to you, as it has come to other women, when success, the applause of the crowd, and a knowledge of great deeds effected will prove a poor consolation for the want of one single human being on whom to lavish a woman's love. Most faculties become smaller by disuse, but it is not so with the affections; they revenge themselves on those who have dared to disbelieve in their force."

"You assume," said Miss Fitzherbert, "that I love your brother."

"Is it not so?"

"No! a thousand times no!"

"You feel that you might love him. That is the dawn of love."

"Listen, Lady Middlesex. That dawn has not opened to me. I will not deny, I have felt a prepossession in favour of your brother; but I have the strongest conviction that my life will be better and happier because of my refusing to give way to it. For me there is no love of the kind. In lonely maidenhood I will live and die. If my choice is unwise, I will be the sufferer; and I have surely the right to make it. My lady, our interview is at an end."

Lady Middlesex rose and bowed her adieu, but another thought seemed to occur to her. "You will," she said, "at least see my brother before he goes. Indeed, otherwise I doubt his leaving. He told me this morning that he would resign."

Miss Fitzherbert after a moment's thought replied, "I will see your brother. Bid him call on me in two hours' time. Goodbye."

As she was left alone a look of agony came over her face. "Am I wise?" she said. "That subtle woman knew how to wound me. She is right. I could love; I could adore the man I loved. Will all the triumphs of the world and the sense of the good I do to others console me during the years to come for the sunshine of love to which every woman has a claim? Yes, I do not deny the claim, high as my conception is of a woman's destiny." After a few moments' pause, she started up indignantly. "Am I then," she exclaimed half aloud, "that detestable thing a woman with a mission, and does the sense of that mission restrain me from yielding to my inclination?" Again she paused, and then resumed, "No, it is not so. I have too easily accepted Lady Middlesex's insinuation. I am neither ambitious nor philanthropic to excess. It is a powerful instinct that speaks to me about Lord Reginald. To a certain extent I am drawn to him, but I doubt him, and it is that which restrains me. I am more disposed to be frightened of than to love him. Why do I doubt him? Some strong impulse teaches me to do so. What do I doubt? I doubt his loving me with a love that will endure, I doubt our proving congenial companions, and—why may I not say it to myself?—I doubt his character. I question his sincerity. The happiness of a few months might be followed by a life of misery. I must be no weak fool to allow myself to be persuaded."

Hilda Fitzherbert was a thoroughly good, true-hearted, and lovable girl. Clever, well informed, and cultivated to the utmost, she had no disposition to prudery or priggishness. She was rather inclined to under- than over-value herself. Lady Middlesex's clever insinuations had caused her for the moment to doubt her own conduct; but reflection returned in time, and once more she became conscious that she felt for Lord Reginald no more attachment than any woman might entertain for a handsome, accomplished man who persistently displayed his admiration. She was well aware that under ordinary circumstances such feelings as she had, might develop into strong love if there were no reverse to the picture; but in this case conviction—call it, if you will, an instinct—persuaded her there was an opposite side. She felt that Lord Reginald was playing a part; that, if his true character stood revealed to her, an unfathomable abyss would yawn between them.

Her reflections were disturbed by the entrance of a lady of very distinguished mien. She might indeed look distinguished, for the Right Honourable Mrs. Hardinge was not only Prime Minister of the empire of Britain, but the most powerful and foremost statesman in the world. In her youth she had been a lovely girl; and even now, though not less than forty years of age, she was a beautiful—it might be more correct to say, a grand—woman. A tall, dignified, and stately figure was set off by a face of which every feature was artistically correct and capable of much variety of expression; and over that expression she held entire command. She had, if she wished it, an arch and winning manner, such as no one but a cultivated Irishwoman possesses; the purest Irish blood ran through her veins. She could say "No" in a manner that more delighted the person whose request she was refusing than would "Yes" from other lips. An adept in all the arts of conversation, she could elicit information from the most inscrutable statesmen, who under her influence would fancy she was more confidential to them than they to her. By indomitable strength she had fought down an early inclination to impulsiveness. The appearance still remained, but no statesman was more slow to form opinions and less prone to change them. She could, if necessary, in case of emergency, act with lightning rapidity; but she had schooled herself to so act only in cases of extreme need. She had a warm heart, and in the private relations of life no one was better liked.

Hilda Fitzherbert worshipped her; and Mrs. Hardinge, childless and with few relations, loved and admired the girl with a strength and tenacity that made their official relations singularly pleasant.

"My dear Hilda," she said, "why do you look so disturbed, and how is it you are idle? It is rare to find you unoccupied."

Hilda, almost in tears, responded, "Dear Mrs. Hardinge, tell me, do tell me, what do you really think of Lord Reginald Paramatta?"

If Mrs. Hardinge felt any surprise at the extraordinary abruptness of the question, she did not permit it to be visible.

"My dear, the less you think of him the better. I will tell you how I read his character. He is unstable and insincere, capable of any exertion to attain the object on which he has set his mind; the moment he has gained it the victory becomes distasteful to him. I have offered him the command of our London forces to please you, but I tell you frankly I did so with reluctance. Nor would I have promoted him to the post but that it has long ceased to possess more than traditional importance. Those chartered sybarites the Londoners can receive little harm from Lord Reginald, and the time has long passed for him to receive any good. Such as it is, his character is moulded; and professionally he is no doubt an accomplished officer and brave soldier. Besides that, he possesses more than the ordinary abilities of a man."

Hilda looked her thanks, but said no more than "Your opinion does not surprise me, and it tallies with my own judgment."

"Dear girl, do not try to dispute that judgment. And now to affairs of much importance. I have come from the Emperor, and I see great difficulties in store for us."

Probably Hilda had never felt so grateful to Mrs. Hardinge as she did now for the few words in which she had expressed so much, with such fine tact. An appearance of sympathy or surprise would have deeply wounded the girl.

"Dear mamma," she said—as sometimes in private in moments of affection she was used to do—"does his Highness still show a disinclination to the settlement to which he has almost agreed?"

"He shows the most marked disinclination, for he told me with strong emotion that he felt he would be sacrificing the convictions of his race."

The position of the Emperor was indeed a difficult one. A young, high-spirited, generous, and brave man, he was asked by his Cabinet to take a step which in his heart he abhorred. A short explanation is necessary to make the case clear. When the Imperial Constitution of Britain was promulgated, women were beginning to acquire more power; but no one thought of suggesting that the preferential succession to the direct heirs male should be withdrawn.

Meanwhile women advanced, and in all other classes of life they gained perfect equality with regard to the laws of succession and other matters, but the custom still remained by which the eldest daughter of the Emperor would be excluded in favour of the eldest son. Some negotiations had proceeded concerning the marriage of the Emperor to the daughter of the lady who enjoyed the position of President of the United States, an intense advocate of woman's equality. She was disposed, if not determined, to make it a condition of the marriage that the eldest child, whether son or daughter, should succeed. The Emperor's Cabinet had the same view, and it was one widely held throughout the Empire. But there were strong opinions on the other side. The increasing number of women elected by popular suffrage to all representative positions and the power which women invariably possessed in the Cabinet aroused the jealous anger of men. True, the feeling was not in the ascendant, and other disabilities of women were removed; but in this particular case, the last, it may be said, of women's disabilities, a separate feeling had to be taken into account. The ultra-Conservatives throughout the Empire, including both men and women, were superstitiously tenacious of upholding the Constitution in its integrity and averse to its being changed in the smallest particular.

They felt that everything important to the Empire depended upon the irrevocable nature of the Constitution, and that the smallest change might be succeeded by the most organic alterations. The merits of the question mattered nothing in their opinion in comparison with the principle which they held it was a matter of life and death not to disturb.

It was now proposed to introduce a Bill to enable the Emperor to declare that the succession should be to the eldest child. The Cabinet were strongly in favour of it, and to a great extent their existence as a Government depended on it. The Emperor was well disposed to his present advisers, but, it was no secret, was strongly averse to this one proposal. The contemplated match was an affair of State policy rather than of inclination. He had seldom met his intended bride, and was not prepossessed with her. She was good-looking and a fine girl; but she had unmistakably red hair, an adornment not to his taste. Besides, she was excessively firm in her opinions as to the superiority of women over men; and he strongly suspected she would be forever striving to rule not only the household, but the Empire. It is difficult to fathom the motives of the human mind, difficult not only to others, but to the persons themselves concerned. The Emperor thought that his opposition to placing the succession on an equality between male and female was purely one of loyalty to his ancestors and to the traditions of the Empire. But who could say that he did not see in a refusal to pass the necessary Act a means of escaping the distasteful nuptials? Mrs. Hardinge had come from a long interview with him, and it was evident that she greatly doubted his continued support. She resumed, "His Highness seems very seriously to oppose the measure, and indeed quite ready to give up his intended marriage. I wonder," she said, looking keenly at Hilda, "whether he has seen any girl he prefers."

The utter unconsciousness with which Hilda heard this veiled surmise appeared to satisfy Mrs. Hardinge; and she continued, "Tell me, dear, what do you think?"

"I am hardly in a position to judge. Does the Emperor give no reasons for his opposition?"

"Yes, he has plenty of reasons; but his strongest appears to be that whoever is ruler of the Empire should be able to lead its armies."

"I thought," said Miss Fitzherbert, "that he had some good reason."

"Do you consider this a good reason?" inquired Mrs. Hardinge sharply.

"From his point of view, yes; from ours, no," said Hilda gently, but promptly.

"Then you do not think that we should retreat from our position even if retreat were possible?"

"No," replied Hilda. "Far better to leave office than to make a concession of which we do not approve in order to retain it."

"You are a strange girl," said Mrs. Hardinge. "If I understand you rightly, you think both sides are correct."

"I think that there is a great deal to be said on both sides, and this is constantly the case with important controversies. Between the metal and the flint the spark of truth is struck. I should think it no disgrace to be defeated on a subject about which we could show good cause. I might even come to think that better cause had been shown against us after the discussion was over; but to flee the discussion, to sacrifice conviction to expediency—that would be disgraceful."

"Then," said Mrs. Hardinge, with some interest, "if the Emperor were to ask your opinion, you would try to persuade him to our side?"

"Yes and no. I would urge strongly my sense of the question and my opinion that it is better to settle at once a controversy about which there is so much difference of opinion. But I should respect his views; and if they were conscientious, I should not dare to advise him to sacrifice them."

An interruption unexpected by Miss Fitzherbert, but apparently not surprising to Mrs. Hardinge, occurred. An aide-de-camp of the Emperor entered. After bowing low to the ladies, he briefly said, "His Imperial Majesty desires the presence of Miss Fitzherbert."

A summons so unusual raised a flush to the girl's cheek. She looked at Mrs. Hardinge.

"I had intended to tell you," said that lady, "that the Emperor mentioned he would like to speak to you on the subject we have been considering." Then, turning to the aide-de-camp, she said, "Miss Fitzherbert will immediately wait on his Majesty."

The officer left the room.

Hilda archly turned to Mrs. Hardinge. "So, dear mamma, you were preparing me for this interview?"

"Dear child," said the elder lady, "you want no preparation. Whatever the consequences to me, I will not ask you to put any restraint on the expression of your opinions."

II

The Emperor and Hilda Fitzherbert

The Emperor received Miss Fitzherbert with a cordial grace, infinitely pleasing and flattering to that young lady. She of course had often seen his Majesty at Court functions, but never before had he summoned her to a separate audience. And indeed, high though her official position and reputation were, she did not hold Cabinet rank; and a special audience was a rare compliment, such as perhaps no one in her position had ever previously enjoyed.

The Emperor was a tall man of spare and muscular frame, with the dignity and bearing of a practised soldier. It was impossible not to recognise that he was possessed of immense strength and power of endurance. He had just celebrated his twenty-seventh birthday, and looked no more than his age. His face was of the fair Saxon type. His eyes were blue, varying with his moods from almost dark violet to a cold steel tint. Few persons were able to disguise from him their thoughts when he fixed on them his eyes, with the piercing enquiry of which they were capable. His eyes were indeed singularly capable of a great variety of expression. He could at will make them denote the thoughts and feelings which he wished to make apparent to those with whom he conversed. Apart from his position, no one could look at him without feeling that he was a distinguished man. He was of a kindly disposition, but capable of great severity, especially towards anyone guilty of a mean or cowardly action. He was of a highly honourable disposition, and possessed an exalted sense of duty. He rarely allowed personal inclination to interfere with public engagements; indeed, he was tenaciously sensitive on the point, and sometimes fancied that he permitted his judgment to be obscured by his prepossessions when he had really good grounds for his conclusions. On the very subject of his marriage he was constantly filled with doubt as to whether his objection to the proposed alteration in the law of succession was well founded on public grounds or whether he was unconsciously influenced by his personal disinclination to the contemplated union. He realised the truth of the saying of a very old author—

"Uneasy lies the head that wears a crown."

After indicating to Miss Fitzherbert his wish that she should be seated, he said to her, "I have been induced to ask your attendance by a long conversation I have had with Mrs. Hardinge. I have heard the opinions she has formed, and they seem to me the result of matured experience. It occurred to me that I would like to hear the opinions of one who, possessed of no less ability, has been less subject to official and diplomatic exigencies. I may gather from you how much of personal feeling should be allowed to influence State affairs."

"Your Majesty is very gracious," faltered Hilda, "but Mrs. Hardinge has already told you the opinion of the Cabinet. Even if I differed from it, which I do not, I could not venture to obtrude my view on your Majesty."

"Yes, you could," said the Emperor, "if I asked you, or let me say commanded you."

"Sir, your wishes are commands. I do not pretend to have deeply studied the matter. I think the time has come to finally settle a long-mooted question and to withdraw from woman the last disability under which she labours."

"My objection," interposed the Emperor, "or hesitation is in no manner caused by any doubt as to woman's deserving to be on a par with man in every intellectual position."

"Then, Sir, may I ask, why do you hesitate? The greatest Sovereign that ever reigned over Great Britain, as it was formerly called, was a woman."

"I cordially agree with you. No Sovereign ever deserved better of the subjects of the realm than my venerated ancestress Queen Victoria. But again I say, I do not question woman's ability to occupy the throne to the greatest advantage."

"Why, may I ask, then does your Majesty hesitate?"

"I can scarcely reply to my own satisfaction. I give great heed to the objections commonly stated against altering the Constitution, but I do not feel certain that these alone guide me. There is another, and to me very important, reason. It appeals to me not as Sovereign only, but as soldier. My father and my grandfather led the troops of the Empire when they went forth to battle. Happily in our day war is a remote contingency, but it is not impossible. We preserve peace by being prepared for war. It seems to me a terrible responsibility to submit to a change which might result in the event of war in the army not being led by its emperor."

"Your Majesty," said Miss Fitzherbert, "what am I to say? To deny the cogency of your reasons is like seeking to retain power, for you know the fate of the Cabinet depends upon this measure, to which it has pledged itself."

"Miss Fitzherbert," said the Emperor gravely, "no one will suspect you of seeking to retain office for selfish purposes, and least of all would I suppose it, or I would not ask your counsel. Tell me now," he said, with a winning look, "as woman to man, not as subject to Sovereign, what does your heart dictate?"

"Sir," said Miss Fitzherbert with great dignity, rising from her seat, "I am deeply sensible of the honour you do me; and I cannot excuse myself from responding to it. In the affairs of life, and more especially State affairs, I have noticed that both sides to a controversy have frequently good grounds for their advocacy; and, moreover, it often happens that previous association fastens on each side the views it holds. I am strong in the belief, we are right in wishing this measure to pass; but since you insist on my opinion, I cannot avoid declaring as far as I, a non-militant woman, can judge, that, were I in your place, I would hold the sentiment you express and refuse my sanction."

Hilda spoke with great fervour, as one inspired. The Emperor scarcely concealed his admiration; but he merely bowed courteously, and ended the interview with the words, "I am greatly indebted to you for your frankness and candour."

III

LORD REGINALD PARAMATTA

As Miss Fitzherbert returned to her room, she did not know whether to feel angry or pleased with herself. She was conscious she had not served the interest of her party or of herself, but she realised that she was placed in a situation in which candour was demanded of her, and it seemed to her that the Emperor was the embodiment of all that was gracious and noble in man.

Her secretary informed her that Lord Reginald Paramatta was waiting to see her by appointment.

Lord Reginald was a man of noticeable presence. Above the ordinary height, he seemed yet taller because of the extreme thinness of his frame. Yet he by no means wore an appearance of delicacy. On the contrary, he was exceedingly muscular; and his bearing was erect and soldierlike. He was well known as a brilliant officer, who had deeply studied his profession. But he was not only known as a soldier: he held a high political position. He had for many years continued to represent an Australian constituency in the Federal Parliament. His naturally dark complexion was further bronzed by exposure to the sun. His features were good and strikingly like those of his sister, the Countess of Middlesex. He had also the same sinister expression. The Paramattas were a very old New South Wales family. They were originally sheep-farmers, or squatters as they used to be called. They owned large estates in New South Wales and nearly half of a thriving city. The first lord was called to the peerage in 1930, in recognition of the immense sums that he had devoted to philanthropic and educational purposes. Lord Reginald was the second son of the third and brother of the fourth peer. He inherited from his mother a large estate in the interior of New South Wales.

Miss Fitzherbert greeted Lord Reginald with marked coolness. "Your sister," she said, "told me you were kind enough to desire to wish me farewell before you left to take the London command, upon which allow me to congratulate you."

"Thanks!" briefly replied his Lordship. "An appointment that places me so far from you is not to my mind a subject of congratulation."

Miss Fitzherbert drew herself up, and with warmth remarked, "I am surprised that you should say this to me."

"You ought not to be surprised," replied Lord Reginald. "My sister told you of my feelings towards you, if indeed I have not already sufficiently betrayed them."

"Your sister must have also told you what I said in reply. Pray, my lord, do not inflict on both of us unnecessary pain."

"Do not mistake my passion for a transitory one. Miss Fitzherbert, Hilda, my life is bound up in yours. It depends on you to send me forth the most happy or the most miserable of men."

"Your happiness would not last. I am convinced we are utterly unsuited to each other. My answer is 'No' in both our interests."

"Do not say so finally. Take time. Tell me I may ask you again after the lapse of some few months."

"To tell you so would be to deceive. My answer can never change."

"You love someone else, then?"

"The question, my lord, is not fair nor seemly, nor have you the right to put it. Nevertheless I will say there is no foundation for your surmise."

"Then why finally reject me? Give me time to prove to you how thoroughly I am in earnest."

"I have not said I doubted it. But no lapse of years can alter the determination I have come to. I hope, Lord Reginald, that you will be happy, and that amidst the distractions of London you will soon forget me."

"That would be impossible, but it will not be put to the test. I shall not go to London. I believe it is your wish that we should be separated."

"I have no wish on the subject. There is nothing more to be said," replied Hilda, with extreme coldness.

"Yes, there is. Do not think that I abandon my hope. I will remain near you. I will not let you forget me. I leave you in the conviction that some day you will give me a different answer. When the world is less kind to you than hitherto, you may learn to value the love of one devoted being. There is no goodbye between us."

Hilda suppressed the intense annoyance that both his words and manner occasioned. She merely remarked, with supreme hauteur, "You will at least be good enough to rid me of your presence here."

Her coldness seemed to excite the fury of Lord Reginald beyond the point of control. "As I live, you shall repent this in the future," he muttered in audible accents.

Shortly afterwards a letter from Lord Reginald was laid before the Premier. He was gratified, he wrote, for the consideration the official appointment displayed; but he could not accept it: his parliamentary duties forbade his doing so. If, he continued, it was considered that his duty as an officer demanded his accepting the offer, he would send in his papers and retire from the service, though of course he would retain his position in the Volunteer force unless the Emperor wished otherwise.

It should be explained that the Volunteer force was of at least equal importance to the regular service. Officers had precedence interchangeably according to seniority. Long since the absurdity had been recognised of placing the Volunteer force on a lower footing than the paid forces. Regular officers eagerly sought to be elected to commands in Volunteer regiments, and the colonel of a Volunteer regiment enjoyed fully as much consideration in every respect as the colonel of any of the paid regiments. The duty of defending all parts of the Empire from invasion was specially assigned to volunteers. The Volunteer force throughout the Empire numbered at least two million, besides which there was a Volunteer reserve force of three quarters of a million, which comprised the best men selected from the volunteers. The vacancies were filled up each year by fresh selections to make up the full number. The Volunteer reserve force could be mobilised at short notice, and was available for service anywhere. Its members enjoyed many prized social distinctions. The regular force of the Empire was comparatively small. In order to understand the availability of the Volunteer reserve force, regard must be had to the immense improvement in education. No child attained man or woman's estate without a large theoretical and practical knowledge of scientific laws and their ordinary application. For example, few adults were so ignorant as not to understand the modes by which motive power of various descriptions was obtained and the principles on which the working depended—each person was more or less an engineer. A hundred years since, education was deemed to be the mastering of a little knowledge about a great variety of subjects. Thoroughness was scarcely regarded, and the superficial apology for preferring quantity to quality was "Education does not so much mean imparting knowledge as training the faculties to acquire it." This plausible plea afforded the excuse for wasting the first twenty years of life of both sexes in desultory efforts to acquire a mastery over the dead languages. "It is a good training to the mind and a useful means of learning the living languages" was in brief the defence for the shocking waste of time.

Early in the last century it fell to the lot of the then Prince of Wales, great-grandfather to the present Emperor, to prick this educational bladder. He stoutly declared that his sons should learn neither Latin nor Greek. "Why," he said, "should we learn ancient Italian anymore than the Italians should learn the dialects of the ancient Britons?"

"There is a Greek and Latin literature," was the reply, "but no literature of ancient Britain."

"Yes," replied the Prince, "there is a literature; but does our means of learning the dead languages enable two persons in ten thousand after years of study to take up promiscuously a Latin or Greek book and read it with ease and comfort? They spend much more time in learning Latin and Greek than their own language, but who ever buys a Latin or Greek book to read when he is travelling?"

"But a knowledge of Latin is so useful in acquiring living languages."

"Fudge!" said this unceremonious prince, who, by the way, was more than an average classical scholar. "If I want to go to Liverpool, I do not proceed there by way of New York. I will back a boy to learn how to speak and read with interest three European languages before he shall be able, even with the aid of a dictionary, to laboriously master the meaning of a Latin book he has not before studied." He continued, "Do you think one person out of fifty thousand who have learnt Greek is so truly imbued with the spirit of the Iliad as are those whose only acquaintance with it is through the translations of Derby, Gladstone, or even Pope? It is partly snobbishness," he proceeded, with increased warmth. "The fact is, it is expensive and wasteful to learn Greek and Latin; and so the rich use the acquirement as another means of walling up class against class. At any rate, I will destroy the fashion; and so that there shall be no loss of learning, I will have every Greek and Latin work not yet translated that can be read with advantage by decent and modest people rendered into the English language, if it cost me a hundred thousand pounds: and then there will be no longer an excuse for the waste of millions on dead languages, to say nothing of the loss occasioned by the want of education in other subjects that is consequent on the prominence given to the so-called classical attainments."

The Prince was equal to his word. Science and art, mathematical and technical acquirements, took the place of the classics; and people became really well informed. Living languages, it was found, could be easily learnt in a few months by personal intercourse with a fluent speaker.

This digression has been necessary to explain how it was that the volunteers were capable of acquiring all the scientific knowledge necessary to the ranks of a force trained to the highest military duties. As to the officers, the position was sufficiently coveted to induce competitors for command in Volunteer regiments to study the most advanced branches of the profession.

It will be understood Lord Reginald, while offering to retire from the regular service, but intending to retain his Volunteer command, really made no military sacrifice, whilst he took up a high ground embarrassing to the authorities. He forced them either to accept his refusal of the London command, and be a party to the breach of discipline involved in a soldier declining to render service wherever it was demanded, or to require his retirement from the regular service, with the certainty of all kinds of questions being asked and surmises made.

It was no doubt unusual to offer him such a splendid command without ascertaining that he was ready to accept it, and there was a great risk of Miss Fitzherbert's name being brought up in an unpleasant manner. Women lived in the full light of day, and several journals were in the habit of declaring that the likes and dislikes of women were allowed far too much influence. What an opportunity would be afforded to them if they could hang ever so slightly Lord Reginald's retirement on some affair of the heart connected with that much-envied young statesman Miss Fitzherbert!

Mrs. Hardinge rapidly realised all the features of the case. "He means mischief, this man," she said; "but he shall not hurt Hilda if I can help it." Then she minuted "Write Lord Reginald that I regret he is unable to accept an appointment which I thought would give him pleasure, and which he is so qualified to adorn." She laughed over this sentence. "He will understand its irony," she thought, "and smart under it." She continued, "Add that I see no reason for his retirement from the regular service. It was through accident he was not consulted before the offer was officially made. I should be sorry to deprive the Empire of his brilliant services. Mark 'Confidential.'" Then she thought to herself, "This is the best way out of it. He has gained to a certain extent a triumph, but he cannot make capital out of it."

IV

Partial Victory

Parliament was about to meet, and the Emperor was to open it with a speech delivered by himself. Much difference of opinion existed as to whether reference should be made to the question of altering the nature of the succession. The Emperor desired that all reference to it should be omitted. He told Mrs. Hardinge frankly he had decided not to agree to an alteration, but he said his greatest pain in refusing was the consciousness that it might deprive him of his present advisers. If the recommendation were formally made, he should be compelled to say that he would not concur until he had recourse to other advisers. He wished her not to impose on him such a necessity.

"But," said Mrs. Hardinge, "your Majesty is asking us to hold office at the expense of our opinions."

"Not so," replied his Majesty. "All pressing need of dealing with the question is over. I have resolved to break off the negotiations with the President of the United States for her daughter's hand. I do not think the union would be happy for either, and I take exception to the strong terms in which the President has urged a change in the succession of our imperial line. You see that the question is no longer an urgent one."

"I hardly know to which direction our duty points," Mrs. Hardinge said. "We think the question urgent whether or not your Majesty marries at once."

"Pray do not take that view. There is another reason. I have determined, as I have said, not to accept such advice without summoning other advisers. In adopting this step, I am strictly within my constitutional rights; and I do not say, if a new Cabinet also recommends an alteration in the law of succession I will refuse to accept the advice. I will never voluntarily decline to recognise the constitutional rights which I have sworn to uphold. So it might be that a change of Cabinet would not alter the result, and then it would be held that I had strained my constitutional power in making the change. I do not wish to appear in this or any other question to hold individual opinions. Frankly I will tell you that I doubt if you have the strength to carry your proposed change even if I permitted you to submit it. If I am correct in my conjecture, the question will be forced on you from the other side; and you will be defeated on it. In that case I shall not have interfered; and, as I have said, I prefer not to do so. So you see, Mrs. Hardinge, that I am selfish in wishing you to hold back the question. It is in my own interest that I do so, and you may dismiss all feeling of compunction."

"Your Majesty has graciously satisfied me that I may do as you suggest without feeling that I am actuated by undue desire to continue in office. I agree with your Majesty the parliamentary result is doubtful. It greatly depends on the line taken by Lord Reginald Paramatta and the forty or fifty members who habitually follow him."

The Emperor's speech was received with profound respect. But as soon as he left the council-chamber a murmur of astonishment ran round. It was generally anticipated that the announcement of the royal marriage would be made.

The Federal Chamber was of magnificent dimensions. It accommodated with comfort the seven hundred and fifty members and one thousand persons besides. The Chamber was of circular shape. A line across the centre divided the portion devoted to the members from that occupied by the audience. The latter were seated tier on tier, but not crowded. The members had each a comfortable chair and a little desk in front, on which he could either write or by the hand telegraph communicate telegrams to his friends outside for retransmission if he desired it. He could receive messages also, and in neither case was the least noise made by the instrument.

The council-chamber possessed astonishing acoustic powers. Vast as were its dimensions, a comparatively feeble voice could be clearly heard at the remotest distance. As soon as some routine business was concluded the leader of the Opposition, a lady of great reputation for statesmanship, rose, and, partly by way of interrogation, expressed surprise that no intimation had been made respecting the future happiness of the reigning family. This was about as near a reference to the person of the Sovereign as the rules of the House permitted. Mrs. Hardinge curtly replied that she had no intimation to make, a reply which was received with a general murmur of amazement. The House seemed to be on the point of proceeding to the ordinary business, when Lord Reginald Paramatta rose and said "he ventured to ask, as no reference was made to the subject in the speech, what were the intentions of the Government on the question of altering the law of succession of the imperial family."

This interruption was received with much surprise. Lord Reginald had long been a member possessed of great influence. He had a considerable following, numbering perhaps not less than fifty. His rule of conduct hitherto had been to deprecate party warfare. He tried to hold the balance, and neither side had yet been able to number him and his following as partisans. That he should lead the way to an attack of an extreme party character seemed most astonishing. The few words that he had uttered were rapidly translated into meaning that he intended to throw in his lot with the Opposition. Mrs. Hardinge, however, appeared to feel no concern as she quietly replied that she was not aware that the question pressed for treatment. "I am afraid," said Lord Reginald, "that I am unable to agree with this opinion; and it is my duty to test the feelings of the House on the subject." Then he read to the intently listening members a resolution of which he gave notice that it was desirable, in order that no uncertainty should exist on the subject, to record the opinion of the House that the law of succession should not be altered. Loud cheers followed the announcement; and the leader of the Opposition, who was equally taken by surprise, congratulated Lord Reginald, with some little irony, on the decided position he had at last assumed. Mrs. Hardinge, without any trace of emotion or anxiety, rose amidst the cheers of her side of the House. The noble and gallant member, she said, had given notice of a resolution which the Government would consider challenged its position. It would be better to take it before proceeding to other business, and if, as she expected, the reply to the Imperial speech would not occasion discussion, tomorrow could be devoted to it. Lord Reginald replied tomorrow would suit him, and the sitting soon came to an end.

Mrs. Hardinge could not but feel surprise at the accuracy of the Emperor's anticipation. She was sure he was not aware of Lord Reginald's intention, and she knew that the latter was acting in revenge for the slight he had received at the hands of Hilda Fitzherbert. She felt that the prospect of the motion being carried was largely increased through Lord Reginald having so cleverly appropriated it to himself. But it was equally evident from the cordiality with which the proposal was received that, if Lord Reginald had not brought it on, someone else would. She saw also that the Countess of Cairo (the leader of the Opposition) had rapidly decided to support Lord Reginald, though she might have reasonably objected to his appropriating the subject. "He is clever," Mrs. Hardinge reflected. "He accurately gauged Lady Cairo's action. What a pity neither Hilda nor I can trust him! He is as bad in disposition as he is able in mind."

The next day, after the routine business was disposed of, Lord Reginald's resolution was called on. That it excited immense interest the crowded state of the hall in every part attested. Two of the Emperor's aides-de-camp were there, each with a noiseless telegraph apparatus in front of him to wire alternately the progress of the debate. Reporters were similarly communicating with the *Argus*, *Age*, and *Telegraph* in Melbourne, and with the principal papers in Sydney, Brisbane, Adelaide, and New Zealand.

Lord Reginald rose amidst loud cheers from the Opposition side of the House. He made a temperate but exceedingly able speech. He would explain before he concluded why he had taken the lead in bringing the question on. Hitherto he had not sought to take a prominent place in politics. He was a soldier by profession, and he would infinitely prefer distinguishing himself as a soldier than as a politician; and, as he would show, it was as a soldier that he came forward. He disclaimed any hostility to the equality of the sexes or any objection to the increasing power in public affairs to which women were attaining. He fully recognised that the immense progress of the world during the last hundred years was largely due to the intellectual advancement of women. He equally rejected the idea that women were unfitted to rule over a constitutionally governed empire.

Then he dwelt at great length on the inexpediency of permitting the Constitution to be altered in anyone particular, and this part of his speech was warmly cheered by a considerable section on each side of the Chamber. The effect of these remarks was, however, marred as far as the Government party were concerned by a sneering reference to their disposition to changes of all kinds; and he attempted a feeble joke by insinuating that the most desirable change of all might be a change of government.

Then he came to his main argument and explained that it was this consideration which had impelled him to take up the question. He was, as he had said, a soldier; but he was not one who overlooked the misery caused by war. He did not long for war, nor did he think that war was a probable contingency; but he felt that the British Empire should always be ready for war as the best means of avoiding it, and as a soldier he believed no greater prestige could be given to the forces of their vast dominions than the knowledge that the Emperor was ready to lead them in person. "I would not," he said, "exclude the female line; but I would not give it larger probabilities of succession than it enjoys at present. Again, as a soldier I declare that the interests of the Empire forbid our doing anything to limit the presence at the head of his forces of the ruler of the Empire."

Lord Reginald sat down amidst cheers. He had been listened to with profound attention, and parts of his speech were warmly applauded. Still, on the whole, the speech was not a success. Everyone felt that there was something wanting. The speaker seemed to be deficient in sincerity. The impression left was that he had some object in view. The malign air with which the little joke was uttered about a change of government was most repelling. It came with singularly bad grace from one who tried to make out that he was unwillingly forced into opposition to a Government with which he had been friendly.

Mrs. Hardinge rose amidst loud and continuous cheers. She combated each argument of the last speaker. She admitted her great disinclination to change the Constitution, but, she asked, was reverence for the Constitution promoted by upholding it on the ground not of its merits, but of the inexpediency of varying it? She freely admitted that her feelings were in favour of changing the laws of succession, but she had not brought forward any proposal to that effect, nor, as an advocate of a change, did she see any immediate or early need of bringing down proposals. Was it a good precedent to make great Ministerial changes depend on resolutions affecting not questions before the House, not proposals made by the Government, but sentiments or opinions they were supposed to entertain? This was a great change in parliamentary procedure, a larger one than those changes which the noble lord had sneeringly credited her with advocating. Then she gave Lord Reginald a very unpleasant quarter of an hour. She pictured him as head of the Government in consequence of carrying his resolution; she selected certain unpopular sentiments which he was known to entertain, and, amidst great laughter, travestied Lord Reginald's defence of his fads in response to resolutions of the same kind as they were now discussing. She grew eloquent even to inspiration in describing the abilities of the female Sovereigns of the past. And as to the soldier's point of view she asked did not history tell them that the arms of the country had been as successful under female as under male rulers? The noble lord, she said, amidst roars of laughter, had intended to come forward as a soldier; but, for her part, she thought he had posed as a courtier, and sarcastically she hinted that he was as able in one capacity as the other. "He is sad, sir," she continued, "over the possibility that anyone but the Emperor should lead the forces; but if all that is said as to the noble lord's ambition be correct, he would prefer leading the troops himself to following the lead of the most exalted commander." She concluded with an eloquent appeal to her own party. She did not deny the opinions of her colleagues and herself, but asked was it wise to allow a great party to be broken up by a theoretical discussion upon a subject not yet before the country, and which for a long while might not come before it? Mrs. Hardinge's speech was received most enthusiastically, and at its conclusion it was clear that she had saved her party from breaking up. Not a vote would be lost to it. The result merely depended on what addition Lord Reginald's own following could bring to the usual strength of the Opposition. After some more debating a division ensued, and the resolution was lost by two votes only. Both sides cheered, but there was breathless silence when Mrs. Hardinge rose. She made no reference to the debate beyond the very significant one of asking that the House should adjourn for a week.

V

CABINET NEGOTIATIONS

M rs. Hardinge tendered the resignation of the Government to the Emperor, who at once sent for Lady Cairo, the leader of the Opposition. He asked her to form an administration.

"Your Majesty," she said, "knows that, though I am in opposition to the present Premier, I greatly admire both her ability and honesty of purpose. I am not at all satisfied that she is called on to resign, or that the small majority she had on the late resolution indicates that she has not a large following on other questions."

"I hold," said the Emperor, "the balance evenly between the great parties of the State; and I respect the functions of the Opposition no less than those of the Government. It is the opinion of my present advisers that a strong administration is necessary, and that, after such a division as that of the other night, the Opposition should have the opportunity offered to them of forming a Government."

"I respect," replied Lady Cairo, "Mrs. Hardinge's action, and under like circumstances would have pursued a like course. But though Mrs. Hardinge is right in offering us the opportunity, it does not follow that we should be wise in accepting it."

"You are of that," replied the Emperor, "of course the best judge. But I should not like so grave a step as the one which Mrs. Hardinge has felt it her duty to take to be construed into a formality for effacing the effect of a vote of the House. I am averse," said the wise ruler, "to anything which might even remotely make me appear as the medium of, or interferer with, parliamentary action. I esteem Mrs. Hardinge, and I esteem you, Lady Cairo; but if the resignation now tendered to me went no further than at present, it might justly be surmised that I had permitted myself to be the means of strengthening what Mrs. Hardinge considered an insufficient parliamentary confidence. I therefore ask you not to give me a hasty answer, but to consult your friends and endeavour to form a strong Government."

No more could be said. Lady Cairo, with becoming reverence, signified her submission to the Emperor's wishes. She summoned her chief friends and colleagues, and had many earnest conferences with them separately and collectively. It was readily admitted that, if they formed a Government, there was a considerable number of members who, though not their supporters, would protect them in a fair trial. It was indeed certain that Mrs. Hardinge would be too generous to indulge in factious opposition, and that, if they avoided any notoriously controversial measure, she would herself help them to get through the session. But Lady Cairo was a large-minded statesman. She loved power, but, because she loved it, was averse to exercising it on sufferance. She could not but be sensible such would be her position, and that she would have to trust less to the strength of her own party than to the forbearance of her opponents. Besides, there was a point about which a great difference of opinion existed. She could not attempt to form a Government unless in combination with Lord Reginald, who moved the resolution. The animosity he had displayed to the Government made it probable, almost certain, that he would do what he could to aid her; it might even be expected that he would induce all or nearly all of his followers to come over to her; but again and again she asked herself the question would such an alliance be agreeable to her? Joint action during an animated debate was widely different from the continued intimacy of official comradeship. She liked Lord Reginald no better than other persons liked him. She had very clear perceptions, and was of a high and honourable nature. Lord Reginald inspired her with distrust. It was his misfortune to awaken that feeling in the minds of those persons with whom he came into contact. Her most trusted colleagues were generally of the same opinion, though several prominent members of the party thought it a mistake not to accept the opportunity and test its chances.

Her intimate friends expressed their opinion with diffidence. They would not accept the responsibility of dissuading her from taking office. They knew that it was a high position and one to which individually she would do justice, and they knew also that many contingencies might convert a Government weak at the outset into a strong one. But she could read between the lines, the more especially that she shared the distrust at which they hinted. Two of the colleagues she most valued went so far as to leave her to understand that they would not join her Government, though of course they would support it. They excused themselves on private grounds; but she was shrewd enough to see these were the ostensible, not the real, reasons. Lady Cairo was not one of those persons who habitually try to persuade themselves to what their inclinations lead. What she had said to the Emperor satisfied the most fastidious loyalty. She was perfectly free to take office. No one could question either her action or her motive. She need not fear the world's opinion if she consulted her own inclination, and nineteen out of twenty persons would have been satisfied. She was not; she still saw before her the necessity of acting with one colleague at least, Lord Reginald, who would be distasteful to her: and as a strong party statesman, she was not well disposed generally to the bulk of his followers, whose inclination led them to endeavour to hold the balance of power between contending parties. She determined on consulting her aged mother, now a confirmed invalid, but once a brilliant and powerful statesman, noted for her high sense of honour.

"My dear," said this helpless lady when she had heard all her daughter had to tell her, "no one but yourself can measure the strength or the justice of the distaste you feel for the alliance you must make if you accept the splendid responsibilities offered to you. But the distaste exists, and it is not likely to become less. I doubt if you are justified in disregarding it. Your time will come, my dear; and it will be a pleasure to you to think that you have not sought it at the expense of a personal sacrifice of doubts, that would not exist if all grounds for them were wanting. You must decide. I will go no further than to say this. I cannot persuade you to allow your inclination for office to overrule your disinclination to a powerful section of those who must share your responsibilities. It is sadly often the case that the instinct to sacrifice inclination is more reliable than the disposition to follow it."

Three days after their last interview the Emperor again received Lady Cairo.

"Your Majesty, I have to decline, with great respect and much gratitude for the confidence you reposed in me, the task of forming a Government with which you graciously charged me."

"Is this your deliberate decision? I am told that you would have no difficulty in carrying on the business of the session if Lord Reginald and his party supported you."

"That is a contingency, Sir, on which I could not count."

"How! He has not promised to support you?"

"I have not asked him. Our chance presence in the same division lobby did not appear to me a sufficient basis of agreement."

"Then," said the Emperor, "the mover of the resolution that has occasioned so much trouble has not been consulted?"

"It is so, your Majesty, as far as I am concerned. I did not understand that you made coalition with him a condition of my attempt to form a Government. I hope, Sir, you acquit me of having disregarded your wishes."

"I do, Lady Cairo. I made no conditions, nor was I entitled to do so. I left you quite free. Only it seemed to me you must act with the support of Lord Reginald and his following, and that therefore you would necessarily consult him."

"I would not say anything in disparagement of Lord Reginald; but may it not be that my party do not think there has been such habitual agreement with him as to warrant our assuming that a coalition would be for the public interest, to say nothing of our own comfort?"

"I see," muttered the Emperor in barely audible voice, "always the same distrust of this man, able and brave though he be." Then aloud, "Lady Cairo, what am I to do? Should I send for Lord Reginald and ask him to attempt to form a Government?"

"I implore your Majesty not to ask me for advice. Mrs. Hardinge is still in power. May I," she said in a tone of pathetic entreaty, "utter half a dozen words not officially, but confidentially?"

"Certainly you have my permission."

"Then, Sir, you will understand me when I say that personal opinions, confidence, trust, and liking may have so much to do with the matter that it will be graciously kind of your Majesty to allow me to state only this much in my place in the House: that, after considering the charge you entrusted to me, I felt compelled to refuse it, not believing that I could form a Government which would enjoy the confidence of a majority of the House."

"Let it be so," said the Emperor good-humouredly. "That may be your version. I must not put my troubles upon you."

"Your Majesty is most good, most kind. I can never be sufficiently grateful."

The Emperor had gained one more devoted admirer. Few who came into personal contact with him failed to be fascinated by his wonderful sympathy and grace. All human character appeared an open book to his discernment.

He sent for Mrs. Hardinge. "I fear," he said, "you will not be pleased at what I am about to say. Lady Cairo has declined to form a Government. I may have to refuse to accept your resignation, or rather to ask you to withdraw it. First, however, I wish your advice; but before I formally seek it tell me would it be distasteful to you to give it."

He paused to afford an opportunity to Mrs. Hardinge to speak, of which she did not avail herself.

"Lady Cairo," he continued, "did not communicate at all with the mover of the resolution, Lord Reginald. Will you be averse to my asking you to advise me on the subject?"

It will be observed that he did not ask for the advice. He well knew, if he did so, Mrs. Hardinge would be bound to declare that he had asked for advice, and whether she gave it or not, would still be unable to conceal that it was sought from her. The Emperor now only put his question on the footing of whether she was willing that he should seek her opinion. Mrs. Hardinge appreciated his consideration. It all came back to the point that the objection to Lord Reginald was of a personal nature, and as such it was in the last degree distasteful to everyone to be mixed up with its consideration.

"Your Majesty," said Mrs. Hardinge, "has a claim to seek my advice on the subject; but there are reasons which make me very averse to giving it. If I can avoid doing so, you will make me very grateful."

The Emperor mused. "Whatever the special reasons may be, why should I force on so valuable a public servant the necessity of making a lifelong enemy of this unscrupulous man? To me his enmity matters little. I will myself decide the point. Lord Reginald did not carry his resolution, and Mrs. Hardinge need not have tendered her resignation. She did offer it; and, guided by constitutional rule, I sent for the leader of the Opposition. I did not take advice from Mrs. Hardinge as to whether I should send for Lord Reginald or Lady Cairo. I acted on my own responsibility, as in such cases I prefer doing. I am opposed to the principle of a retiring Minister selecting his or her successor. I had the right to suppose that Lady Cairo would consult Lord Reginald, though not to complain of her failing to do so. If I send for Lord Reginald, it must be of my own initiative. There is no reason why I should consult Mrs. Hardinge now, seeing that I did not consult her at first. So much then is settled. Now I must myself decide if I will send for Lord Reginald. It will be distasteful to me to do so. I have no confidence in the man, and it would be a meaningless compliment, for he cannot form a Government. Why should I make a request I know cannot be complied with? Constitutional usage does not demand it; in fact, the precedent will be injurious. Because of a sudden accidental combination, the representative of a small party has no right to be elevated into the most important leader. Such a practice would encourage combinations injurious to party government. If I had intended to send for Lord Reginald, I ought to have summoned him before I sought Lady Cairo. I am quite satisfied that the course I pursued was constitutional and wise, and I should throw doubt upon it by sending for Lord Reginald now." These reflections were made in less time than it takes to write them down.

"Mrs. Hardinge," said the Emperor, "we now begin our official interview. Be kind enough to efface from your mind what has hitherto passed. I have to ask you to withdraw your resignation. Lady Cairo, the leader of the Opposition, has declined to act, on the ground that she cannot form a Government which will sufficiently possess the confidence of a majority of the House."

"It shall be as your Majesty wishes," said Mrs. Hardinge.

When the House met, Mrs. Hardinge, by agreement with Lady Cairo, merely stated that, after the division of last week, she had felt it her duty to tender the resignation of her Government to the Emperor.

Lady Cairo in very few words explained that the Emperor had sent for her and entrusted her with the formation of a Government, and that, after sufficient consideration, she resolved it was not desirable she should undertake the task, as she could not rely on a majority in the House and could not submit to lead it on sufferance.

Mrs. Hardinge again rose, and explained that, at the request of the Emperor, she had withdrawn her resignation. Loud cheers from all sides of the House followed the intimation.

Public feeling during the week had abundantly shown itself to be against a change of government upon what really amounted to a theoretical question, as the matter was not before the House upon which the resolution was nearly carried. It was argued that even if carried it would have been a most unsatisfactory reason for a change of government.

There was one member in the Chamber to whom all that had passed was gall and wormwood. Lord Reginald left the House last week a marked and distinguished man. For the first twenty-four hours he received from those persons throughout the Empire who made it their business to stand well with "the powers that be" congratulations of a most flattering description. Today there was "none so poor to do him reverence."

The change was intolerable to a man of his proud and haughty disposition. The worst feature of it was that he could not single out anyone specially for complaint. There was no disguising from himself what everyone in the House knew, and what everyone throughout the Empire soon would know: that the Emperor himself and the leaders of both the great parties did not think him worthy of consideration. As we have seen, there was no actual slight; that is to say, constitutional usages had been followed. But to his mind he had been slighted in a most marked and offensive fashion. Why was he not sent for at first? Why did not Lady Cairo consult him? Why was Mrs. Hardinge asked to withdraw her resignation without his assistance being sought—he, the mover of the resolution; he, the man who brought on the crisis about which miles of newspaper columns had since been written? He forgot that no one had asked him to take the action he did, that he had sought no advice on the subject, and that politicians who elect to act on their own account have no right to complain of the isolation they court. Scarcely anyone spoke to him. A member near him, noticing his extreme pallor, asked him if he was unwell; but no one seemed to care about him or to remember that he had had anything to do with the crisis which, to the rejoicing of all sides, was over. "The newspapers," he thought, "will not forget." They had blamed him during the last week; now they would ridicule and laugh at him. He writhed at the reflection; and when he reached the quiet of his own home, he paced his large study as one demented. "I will be revenged," he muttered over and over again. "I will show them I am not so powerless a being; they shall all repent the insult they have put on me: and as for that girl, that image of snow—she has set Mrs. Hardinge against me. She shall grovel at my feet; she shall implore me to marry her."

VI

BAFFLED REVENGE

Hilda's most confidential secretary was her sister, Maud Fitzherbert. She was some two or three years younger, a lovely, graceful girl, and possessed of scarcely less intellectual power than Hilda. She had perhaps less inclination for public life; but both the girls were learned in physical laws, in mathematics, in living languages, in everything, in short, to which they devoted their extraordinary mental powers. They adored each other, and Maud looked up to Hilda as to a divinity.

The latter was writing in her room. Maud came to her. "Lord Montreal is most anxious to see you for a few minutes."

Lord Montreal was a fine-looking, handsome young man of twenty-five years of age. He was a brave soldier, a genial companion, and a general favourite. He was the second son of the Duke of Ontario. He had known the Fitzherberts since they were children, and the families were intimate. Hilda greeted him cordially.

"I will not detain you," he said; "but I have had important information confided to me in strict secrecy. I cannot tell you who was my informant, and you must not use my name. Will you accept the conditions?"

"I must, I suppose, if you insist on them."

"I must insist on them. My information much concerns my commanding officer, Lord Reginald Paramatta, with whom I am only on formal terms; and therefore my name must not appear. As to my informant, his condition was absolute secrecy as to his name. The gist of what he told me was that Lord Reginald is organising a secret society, with objects certainly not loyal to the Emperor, if indeed they are not treasonable. I gathered that there is something more contemplated than theoretical utterances, and that action of a most disastrous character may follow if steps to arrest it be not at once taken. The information was imparted to me in order that I might bring it to you. I feel that I have been placed in a false position by being made the recipient without proof of statements so damaging to my superior officer; and though I fear that I may be placing a trouble upon you, I have on reflection not thought myself warranted in withholding the statement, as it was made to me with the object of its reaching you. Never again will I give assurances about statements the nature of which I do not know."

Miss Fitzherbert seemed to be destined to annoyance through Lord Reginald. She was now called to set the detective power in force against a man who a few days since so eagerly sought her hand.

"I certainly wish," she said, "that you will not give promises which will land you into bringing me information of this kind."

"You surely," said Montreal, "do not care for Lord Reginald?"

"I may not and do not care for him, but it is not agreeable to be asked to search out criminal designs on the part of a person with whom one is acquainted."

"Forgive me, Hilda," said Montreal. "It was thoughtless of me not to think that I might give you pain. But, you see, I regard you as indifferent to everything but public affairs. Now Maud is different"; and he looked at the fair girl who still remained in the room, with eyes in which warm affection was plainly visible.

"Maud has a heart, of course; but I have not," said Hilda, with more irritation than she was accustomed to display.

The poor girl had suffered much annoyance during the last few days, and the climax was attained that afternoon when she read in a paper purposely sent to her a strangely inverted account of her relations with Lord Reginald. According to this journal, Mrs. Hardinge had treated Lord Reginald cruelly because she could not induce him to respond to the affection which her protégée Hilda Fitzherbert felt for the great soldier. In spite of, or perhaps on account of, her vast mental power, Hilda was possessed of a singularly sensitive character. She gave herself up to public affairs in the full conviction that women could do so without sacrificing in the smallest degree their self-respect. She had a high conception of the purity and holiness of woman's individual existence, and it seemed to her a sacrilege to make the public life of a woman the excuse for dragging before the eyes of the world anything that affected her private feelings. She was intensely annoyed at this paragraph. In the end, we may say in anticipation. Lord Reginald did not come out of it with advantage. The next issue of the paper contained the following passage: "In reference to what appeared in our columns last week about Miss Fitzherbert, we must apologise to that lady. We are informed by Mrs. Hardinge that the facts were absolutely inverted. It is not Lord Reginald who is unwilling. It is Lord Reginald who has received a *decidedly* negative reply."

Hilda was not one to readily inflict her own annoyances on others. She recovered herself in a moment as she saw the pained look on Maud's face. "Forgive me, Montreal; forgive me, Maud," she said. "I have much to disturb me. I did not mean to be unkind. Of course, Montreal, I should have liked your aid in this matter; but as you cannot give it, I must see what I can do without it. Goodbye, Montreal. Maud dear, send at once to Colonel Laurient, and ask him if he will do me the kindness to come to see me at once."

Colonel Laurient was a very remarkable man. He was on his mother's side of an ancient Jewish family, possessing innumerable branches all over the world. At various times members of the family had distinguished themselves both in public life and in scientific, commercial, and financial pursuits. Colonel Laurient was the second son of one of the principal partners in the De Childrosse group, the largest and most wealthy financial house in the world. When his education was completed, he decided not to enter into the business, as his father gave him the option of doing. He had inherited an enormous fortune from his aunt, the most celebrated scientific chemist and inventor of her day. She had left him all the law permitted her to leave to one relation. He entered the army, and also obtained a seat in Parliament. As a soldier he gained a reputation for extreme skill and discretion in the guerilla warfare that sometimes was forced on the authorities in the British Asiatic possessions. On one occasion by diplomatic action he changed a powerful foe on the frontier of the Indian possessions to a devoted friend, his knowledge of languages and Asiatic lore standing him in good stead. This action brought him to the notice of the Emperor, who soon attached him to his personal service, and, it was said, put more faith in his opinions than in those of any person living. He was rather the personal friend than the servant of the Emperor.

Some twenty years before the date of our story it was found necessary to give to the then Sovereign a private service of able and devoted men. It was the habit of the Emperor of United Britain to travel about the whole of his vast dominions. The means of travelling were greatly enlarged, and what would at one time have been considered a long and fatiguing expedition ceased to possess any difficulty or inconvenience. A journey from London to Melbourne was looked upon with as much indifference as one from London to the Continent used to be. It became apparent that either the freedom of the Emperor to roam about at pleasure must be much curtailed, or that he must be able to travel without encroaching on the ordinary public duty of his constitutional advisers. Thus a species of personal bodyguard grew up, with the members of which, according as his temperament dictated, the Sovereign became on more or less intimate personal terms. The officers holding this coveted position had no official status. If there was any payment, the Emperor made it. There was no absolute knowledge of the existence of the force, if such it could be called, or of who composed it. That the Sovereign had intimate followers was of course known, and it was occasionally surmised that they held recognised and defined positions. But it was merely surmise, after all; and not half a dozen people outside of Cabinet rank could have positively named the friends of the Emperor who were members of the bodyguard.

Colonel Laurient retired from Parliament, where he had rather distinguished himself in the treatment of questions requiring large geographical and historical knowledge; and it was commonly supposed, he wished to give more attention to his military duties. In reality he became chief of the Emperor's bodyguard, and, it might be said, was the eyes and ears of the Sovereign. With consummate ability he organised a secret intelligence department, and from one end of the dominions to the other he became aware of everything that was passing. Not infrequently the Emperor amazed Cabinet Ministers with the extent of his knowledge of immediate events. Colonel Laurient never admitted that he held any official position, and literally he did not hold any such position. He received no pay, and his duties were not defined. He loved the Emperor personally for himself, and the Emperor returned the feeling. Really the most correct designation to give to his position was to term him the Emperor's most devoted friend and to consider that in virtue thereof the members of the bodyguard regarded him as their head, because he stood to them in the place of the Emperor himself.

Hilda Fitzherbert knew something, and conjectured more, as to his position. She was frequently brought into communication with him, and after she heard Lord Montreal's story she instantly determined to consult him. He came quickly on her invitation. He was always pleased to meet her.

Colonel Laurient was a tall, slender man, apparently of about thirty-five years of age. His complexion was very dark; and his silky, curly hair was almost of raven blackness. His features were small and regular, and of that sad but intellectual type common to some of the pure-bred Asiatic races. You would deem him a man who knew how to "suffer and be strong"; you would equally deem him one whom no difficulty could frighten, no obstacle baffle. You would expect to see his face light up to enjoyment not because of the prospect of ordinary pleasure, but because of affairs of exceeding gravity which called for treatment by a strong hand and subtle brain. His manner was pleasing and deferential; and he had a voice of rare harmony, over which he possessed complete control. Cordial greetings passed between him and Miss Fitzherbert. There was no affectation of apology being necessary for sending for him or of pleasure on his part at the summons. Briefly she told him of Lord Montreal's communication. He listened attentively, then carelessly remarked, "Lord Reginald's conduct has been very peculiar lately."

Do what she would, the girl could not help giving a slight start at this remark, made as it was with intention. Colonel Laurient at once perceived that there was more to be told than he already was aware of. He knew a great deal that had passed with Lord Reginald, and guessed more; and gradually, with an apparently careless manner, he managed to elicit so much from Hilda that she thought it wiser to tell him precisely all that had occurred, especially the account of her last interview with Lord Reginald and his subsequent letter resigning his appointment.

"Confidences with me," he said, "are entirely safe. Now I understand his motives, you and I start on fair terms, which we could not do whilst you knew more than I did."

Then they discussed what had better be done. "It may be," Colonel Laurient said, "that there is nothing in it. There is a possibility that it is a pure invention, and it is even possible that Lord Reginald may have himself caused the invention to reach you for the purpose of giving you annoyance. Montreal's informant may have been instigated by Lord Reginald. Then there is the possibility—we may say probability— that the purposes of the society do not comprise a larger amount of disaffection or dissatisfaction than the law permits. And, lastly, there is let us say the barest possibility that Lord Reginald, enraged to madness, may have determined on some really treasonable action. You know in old days it was said, 'Hell has no fury like a woman scorned'; but in our time we would not give the precedence for wounded vanity to woman; man is not wanting in the same susceptibility, and Lord Reginald has passed through a whole series of humiliating experiences. I knew some of them before I saw you this afternoon. You have filled up the list with a bitter from which he doubtless suffers more than from all the rest."

Miss Fitzherbert appeared to care little for this strain of conjecture. "What is the use of it?" she said. "However infinitesimal the risk of treasonable designs, the Emperor must not be allowed to run it."

"You are right," said Colonel Laurient. "I do not, as you know, appear in these matters; but I have means of obtaining information of secret things. Within twenty-four hours I will see you again and let you know what it all means. We can then decide the course to take."

Some explanation is necessary to enable Colonel Laurient's remarks about the limits of disaffection to be understood. Freedom of thought and expression was amongst the cardinal liberties of the subject most prized. In order to recognise its value, it was long since determined that a line should be drawn beyond which the liberty should not extend. It was argued that nothing could be more cruel than to play with disaffection of a dangerous nature. Not only was it the means of increasing the disaffection, but of gradually drawing eminent people into compromising positions. The line then was drawn at this point:— upon any subject that did not affect the fundamental principles of the Constitution change might be permissible, but any advocacy or even suggestion of destroying those fundamental principles was regarded as treasonable. The Constitution was so framed as to indicate within itself the principles which were susceptible of modification or change, such, for example, as the conditions of the franchise and the modes of conducting elections. But there were three fundamental points concerning which no change was allowable, and these were—first, that the Empire should continue an empire; secondly, that the sovereignty should remain in the present reigning family; and thirdly, that the union of the different parts of the dominion was irrevocable and indissoluble. It will be remembered that a great aversion had been expressed by the upholders of the Constitution to the proposal to change the law of succession within the imperial family. It could not be said to touch on the second fundamental principle, as it did not involve a change of dynasty; yet many thought it too nearly approached one of the sacred, unchangeable principles.

As regards the fundamental principles, no discussion was permissible. To question even the wisdom of continuing the Empire, of preserving the succession in the imperial family, or of permitting a separation of any of the dominions was held to be rank treason; and no mercy was shown to an offender. Outside of these points changes could be made, and organisations to promote changes were legitimate, however freely they indulged in plain speech. The conduct of the Emperor himself was legitimately a subject of comment, especially on any point in which he appeared to fail in respect to the Constitution he had sworn to uphold. It need scarcely be said that the Constitution was no longer an ill-defined and unwritten one. Such a Constitution worked well enough as long as the different parts of the Empire were united only during pleasure. When the union became irrevocable, it was a natural necessity that the conditions of union should be defined.

It may be convenient here to state some of the broad features of the governing and social system. It has already been said that, without approaching to communism, it had long since been decided that every human being was entitled to a share in the good things of the world, and that destitution was abhorrent. It was also recognised that the happiest condition of humanity was a reasonable amount of work and labour. For that very reason, it was decided not to make the labour distasteful by imposing it as a necessity. The love of work, not its necessity, was the feeling it was desirable to implant. Manual work carried with it no degradation, and there was little work to be done which did not require intelligence. Mere brute force was superseded by the remarkable contrivances for affording power and saving labour which were brought even to the humblest homes. The waves, tides, and winds stored up power which was convertible into electricity or compressed air; and either of these aids to labour-saving could be carried from house to house as easily as water. If men and women wished to be idle and State pensioners, it was open to them to follow their inclination; but they had to wear uniforms, and they were regarded as inferior by the healthy body politic. The aged, infirm, and helpless might enjoy State aid without being subjected to such a humiliation or to any disability. The starting-point was that, if a person was not sufficiently criminal to be the inmate of a prison, he should not be relegated to a brutal existence. It was at first argued that such a system would encourage inaction and idleness; the State would be deluged with pensioners. But subtler counsels prevailed. Far-seeing men and women argued that the condition of the world was becoming one of contracted human labour; and if the viciously inclined refused to work, there would be more left to those who had the ambition to be industrious. "But," was the rejoinder, "you are stifling ambition by making the lowest round of the ladder so comfortable and luxurious." To this was replied, "Your argument is superficial. Survey mankind; and you will see that, however lowly its lowest position, there is a ceaseless, persistent effort to rise on the part of nearly every well-disposed person, from the lowliest to the most exalted." Ambition, it was urged, was natural to man, but it was least active amongst the poverty-crushed classes. Mankind as a whole might be described as myriads of units striving to ascend a mountain. The number of those contented to rest on the plateaus to which they had climbed was infinitesimal compared with the whole. It would be as difficult to select them as it would be to pick out a lazy bee from a whole hive. Whether you started at the lowest class, with individuals always on the point of starvation, with families herded together with less decency than beasts of the fields, and with thousands of human beings who from cradle to grave knew not what happiness meant, or made the start from a higher elevation, upon which destitution was impossible, there would still continue the climbing of myriads to greater heights and the resting on plateaus of infinitesimally few; indeed, as poverty tended to crush ambition, there would be a larger range of aspiration accompanying an improvement in the condition of the lowliest class. And so it proved.

The system of government and taxation followed the theory of the range above destitution. Taxes were exacted in proportion to the ability to pay them. The payments for the many services the Post Office rendered were not regarded as taxation. The customs duties were looked upon as payments made in proportion to the desires of the people to use dutiable goods. If high customs duties meant high prices, they also meant high wages.

The Empire, following the practice of other countries, was utterly averse to giving employment to the peoples of foreign nations. Every separate local dominion within the Empire was at liberty to impose by its legislature what duties it pleased as between itself and other parts of the Empire, but it was imperatively required to collect three times the same duties on commodities from foreign countries. This was of course meant to be prohibitive of foreign importations, and was practicable because the countries within the Empire could supply every commodity in the world. It was argued that to encourage foreign importations merely meant to pit cheap labour against the price for labour within the Empire. Besides the customs duties, the revenue was almost entirely made up of income tax and succession duties. Stamp duties, as obstacles to business, were considered an evidence of the ignorance of the past. The first five hundred pounds a year of income was free; but beyond that amount the State appropriated one clear fourth of all incomes. Similarly one quarter of the value of all successions, real or personal, in excess of ten thousand pounds, was payable to the State; and disposition by gifts before death came within the succession values. A man or woman was compelled to leave half his or her property, after payment of succession duty, in defined proportion to the children and wife or husband, as the case might be, or failing these to near relations; the other half he or she might dispose of at pleasure. It was argued that to a certain extent the amasser of wealth had only a life interest in it, and that it was not for the happiness of the successors of deceased people to come into such wealth that the ambition to work and labour would be wanting. The system did not discourage the amassment of wealth; on the contrary, larger fortunes were made than in former times. Higher prices gave to fortunes of course a comparatively less purchasing power; but taking the higher prices into consideration, the accumulation of wealth became a more honourable ambition and a pleasanter task when it ceased to be purchased at the expense of the comfort of the working classes.

The customs duties belonged to the separate Governments that collected them, and the quarter-income tax and succession duties were equally divided between the Imperial and the Dominion Governments. Thus the friction between them was minimised. The Imperial Government and the Dominion Governments both enjoyed during most years far more revenue than they required, and so large a reserve fund was accumulated that no inconvenience was felt in years of depression. Part of the surplus revenues arising from the reserve fund was employed in large educational and benevolent works and undertakings. The result of the system was that pecuniary suffering in all directions was at an end; but the ambition to acquire wealth, with its concomitant powers, was in no degree abated.

Of course there was not universal content—such a condition would be impossible—but the controversies were, as a rule, less bitter than the former ones which prevailed between different classes. The man-and-woman struggle was one of the large points of constant difference, and again there was much difference of opinion as to whether the quarter-income and succession duties might be reduced to a fifth. It was argued, on the one hand, that the reserve funds were becoming too large, and that the present generation was working too much for its successors. On the other hand, it was urged that the present generation in working for its successors was merely perpetuating the gift which it had inherited, and that by preserving the reserve funds great strength was given to contend against any reverses that the future might have in store. Another point of controversy was the strength of the naval and military forces. A comparatively small school of public men argued that the cost and strength might be materially reduced without risk or danger, but the general feeling was not with them.

This has been a long digression, but it was necessary to the comprehension of our story. It will easily be understood from what has been said that, supposing the alleged action of Lord Reginald was dictated by revenge, it was difficult to see, unless he resorted to treasonable efforts, what satisfaction he could derive from any agitation.

Colonel Laurient the next afternoon fulfilled his promise of waiting on Hilda. She had suffered great anxiety during the interval—the anxiety natural to ill-defined fears and doubts. He looked careworn, and his manner was more serious than on the previous day. "I have found out all about it," he said; "and I am sorry there is more cause for anxiety than we thought yesterday. It is undoubtedly true that Lord Reginald is organising some combination; and although the proof is wanting, there is much reason to fear that his objects are not of a legitimate nature. It is impossible to believe, he would take the trouble which he is assuming, to deal only with questions to which he has never shown an inclination. I am persuaded that behind the cloak of his ostensible objects lies ambition or revenge, or perhaps both, pointing to extreme and highly dangerous action."

"You are probably right," said Miss Fitzherbert, who knew from the manner of the Emperor's favourite that he was much disturbed by what he had heard. "But even so, what obstacle lies in the way of putting an end to the projected action, whatever its nature?"

"There is a great obstacle," promptly replied the Colonel; "and that is the doubt as to what the nature of the project is. Lord Reginald is a clever man; and notwithstanding his late failure, he has plenty of friends and admirers, especially among his own sex, and amongst soldiers, both volunteers and regulars. I have ascertained enough to show me that the leaders intend to keep within ostensibly legitimate limits until the time comes to unfold their full design to their followers, and that then they will trust to the comradeship of the latter and to their fears of being already compromised."

Hilda was quick of apprehension. "I see they will organise to complain perhaps of the nature of the taxation, and only expose their treasonable objects at a later time."

Colonel Laurient gazed on her with admiration. "How readily you comprehend!" he said. "I believe you alone can grapple with the situation."

The girl flushed, and then grew pale. She did not know what physical fear meant. Probably, if her feelings were analysed, it would have been found that the ruling sensation she experienced was an almost delirious pleasure at the idea that she could do a signal service to the Emperor.

She replied, however, with singular self-repression. "I am not quick enough," she said, with a slight smile, "to understand how I can be of any use."

"The organisation has been proceeding sometime, although I fancy Lord Reginald has only lately joined and accepted the leadership. It numbers thousands who believe themselves banded together only to take strong measures to reduce taxation, on the ground that the reserve funds have become amply large enough to permit such reduction. But the leaders have other views; and I have ascertained that they propose to hold a meeting three days hence, at which it is possible—nay, I think, probable—there will be an unreserved disclosure."

"Why not," said Miss Fitzherbert, "arrest them in the midst of their machinations?"

"There lies the difficulty," responded the Colonel. "It entirely depends on the nature of the disclosures whether the Government authorities are entitled to take any action. If the disclosures fall short of being treasonable, it would be held that there was interference of a most unpardonable character with freedom of speech and thought; and the last of it would never be heard. Dear Miss Fitzherbert," he said caressingly, "we want someone at the meeting with a judgment so evenly balanced and accurate that she will be able on the instant to decide if the treasonable intentions are sufficiently expressed or if it would be safer not to interfere. I know no one so quick and at the same time so logical in her judgment as you. In vain have I thought of anyone else whom it would be nearly so safe to employ."

"But how could it be managed?" inquired Hilda. "Everyone knows my appearance. My presence would be immediately detected."

"Pray listen to me," said the Colonel, delighted at having met with no strenuous opposition. He had feared, he would have great difficulty in persuading Miss Fitzherbert to take the part he intended for her;

and, to his surprise, she seemed inclined to meet him half-way. Then he explained that the meeting was to be held in the Parliamentary Hall, a celebrated place of meeting. It had been constructed with the express purpose of making it impossible that anyone not inside the Hall could hear what was taking place. The edifice was an enormous one of stone. Inside this building, about fifteen feet from the walls all round, and twenty feet from the roof, was a second erection, composed entirely of glass. So that as long as the external building was better lighted than the interior one the presence of a human being could be detected outside the walls or on the roof of the hall of meeting. The chamber was artificially cooled, as indeed were most of the houses in the cities of Australia, excepting during the winter months.

"This is the place of all others," said Miss Fitzherbert, "where it would be difficult for an unauthorised person to be present."

"Not so," replied Colonel Laurient. "The inside hall is to be in darkness, and the exterior dimly lighted. Only the vague outlines of each person's form will be revealed; and everyone is to come cloaked, and with a large overshadowing hat. From what I can gather, the revelation is to be gradual and only to be completed if it should seem to be approved during its progress. I expect Lord Reginald will be the last to give in his adhesion, so that it might be said he was deceived as to the purpose of the meeting if he should see fit to withdraw from the declaration of its real object. Mind, you are to be sole judge as to whether the meeting transgresses the line which divides the legitimate from the treasonable."

"Why not act yourself?" said Hilda.

"If you think for a moment," he replied, "you will understand my influence is maintained only so long as it is hidden. If I appeared to act, it would cease altogether. Unfortunately I must often let others do what I would gladly do myself. Believe me, it is painful to me to put tasks on you of any kind, much less a task of so grave a nature. By heavens!" he exclaimed, carried away for a moment, "there is a reason known to me only why I might well dread for myself the great service you will do the Emperor."

He was recalled to himself by the amazed look of the girl. "Forgive me," he exclaimed. "I did not mean anything. But there is no danger to you; of that be assured."

"Colonel Laurient," said Hilda gravely, "you ought to know me well enough not to suppose I am guided by fear."

"I do know it," he answered, "otherwise I should not have asked you to undertake the great task I have set before you. No woman whose mind was disturbed by alarm could do justice to it."

He told her that in some way, he did not mention how, he had control over the manager of the building, who had let it under a false impression, and asked her if she was aware of the comparatively late discovery of how to produce artificial magnetism.

"I ought to be," she replied, with a smile, "for I am credited with having been the first to discover the principle of the remote branch of muscular magnetising electricity on which it depends."

"I had forgotten," he said, with an answering smile. "One may be forgiven for forgetting for a moment the wide nature of your investigations and discoveries."

Then he explained to her that the principle could be put into practice with perfect certainty and safety, and that he would take care everything was properly arranged. He would see her again and tell her the pass-words, the part of the Hall she was to occupy, and the mode she was to adopt to summon assistance.

The evening of the meeting came, and for half an hour there were numerous arrivals at the many doors of the huge building. Each person had separately to interchange the pass-words at both the outer and inner doors. At length about twelve hundred people were assembled. The lights outside the glass hall were comparatively feeble. The powerful electric lamps were not turned on. The inner hall was unlighted, and received only a dull reflection from the outer lights. Some surprise was expressed by the usual frequenters of the Hall at the appearance inside the glass wall of a wooden dais, sufficiently large to hold three or four people, and with shallow steps on one side leading up to it. Inquiry was made as to its object. The doorkeeper, suitably instructed, replied carelessly it was thought, they might require a stage from which the speakers could address the audience. The present meeting certainly did not want it. The speakers had no desire to individually bring themselves into notice. Hilda, muffled up as were the rest, quietly took a seat close to the steps of the dais. No president was appointed; no one appeared to have any control; yet as the meeting proceeded it was evident that its tactics had been carefully thought out, and that most, if not all, of the speakers were fulfilling the parts allotted to them.

First a tall, elderly man rose, and with considerable force and fluency enlarged upon the evils of the present large taxation. He went into figures, and his speech ought to have been effective, only no one seemed to take any interest in it. Then there loomed on the meeting the person apparently of a middle-aged woman. The cloaks and hats carefully mystified the identities of the sexes and individual peculiarities. This speaker went a little further. She explained that maintaining the Empire as a whole entailed the sacrifice of regulating the taxation so as to suit the least wealthy portions. She carefully guarded herself from being more than explanatory. The comparative poverty of England and the exactions of the self-indulgent Londoners, she said, necessitated a scale of taxation that hardy and rich Australia, New Zealand, and Canada did not require. Then a historically disposed young woman rose and dwelt upon the time when England thought a great deal more of herself than of the Colonies and to curry favour with foreign countries placed them on the same footing as her own dominions. Little by little various speakers progressed, testing at every step the feelings of the audience, until at last one went so far as to ask the question whether the time would ever come when Australia would be found to be quite large and powerful enough to constitute an empire of itself. "Mind," said he, "I do not say the time will come." Then an apparently excited Australian arose. She would not, she said, say a word in favour of such an empire; but she, an Australian bred and born, and with a long line of Australian ancestors, was not going to listen to any doubts being thrown on Australia or Australians. The country and the people, she declared, amidst murmuring signs of assent, were fit for any destiny to which they might be called. Then a logical speaker rose and asked why were they forbidden to discuss the question as to whether it was desirable to retain the present limits of the Empire or to divide it. He would not state what his opinion was, but he would say this: that he could not properly estimate the arguments in favour of preserving the integrity of the Empire unless he was at liberty to hear the arguments and answer them of those who held an opposite opinion. When this speaker sat down, there was a momentary pause. It seemed as if there was a short consultation between those who were guiding the progress of the meeting. Whether or not this was the case, some determination appeared to be arrived at; and a short, portly man arose and said he did not care for anybody or anything. He would answer the question to which they had at length attained by saying that in his opinion the present empire was too large, that Australia ought to be formed into a separate empire, and that she would be quite strong enough to take care of herself.

The low murmur of fear with which this bold announcement was heard soon developed into loud cheers, especially from that part of the Hall where the controlling influence seemed to be held. Then all restraint was cast aside; and speaker after speaker affirmed, in all varieties of eloquence, that Australia must be an empire. Some discussed whether New Zealand should be included, but the general opinion appeared to be that she should be left to her own decision in the matter. Then the climax was approached. A speaker rose and said there appeared to be no doubt in the mind of the meeting as to the Empire of Australia; he hoped there was no doubt that Lord Reginald Paramatta should be the first Emperor. The meeting seemed to be getting beyond the control of its leaders. It did not appear to have been part of their programme to put forward Lord Reginald's name at this stage. It was an awkward fix, for no person by name was supposed to be present, so that he could neither disclaim the honour nor express his thanks for it. One of the controllers, a grave, tall woman, long past middle age, dealt with this difficulty. They must not, she said, go too far at first; it was for them now to say whether Australia should be an empire. She loved to hear the enthusiasm with which Lord Reginald Paramatta's name was received. Australia boasted no greater or more distinguished family than the Paramattas; and as for Lord Reginald, everyone knew that a braver and better soldier did not live. Still they must decide on the Empire before the Emperor, and each person present must answer the question was he or she favourable to Australia being constructed into a separate empire? They could not in this light distinguish hands held up. Each person must rise and throw off his or her cloak and hat and utter the words, "I declare that I am favourable to Australia being constituted an empire." Then, evidently with the intention of making the controllers and Lord Reginald speak last, she asked the occupant of the seat to the extreme left of the part of the Hall most distant from her to be the first to declare. Probably he and a few others had been placed there for that purpose. At any rate, he rose without hesitation, threw off his cloak, removed his hat, and said, "I declare myself in favour of Australia being constituted an empire." Person after person from left to right and from right to left of each line of chairs followed the same action and uttered the same words, and throughout the Hall there was a general removal of cloaks and hats. At length it came to Hilda Fitzherbert's turn. Without a moment's hesitation, the brave girl rose, dropped her cloak and hat, and in a voice distinctly heard from end to end of the Hall said, "I declare I am not in favour of Australia being constituted an empire."

For a second there was a pause of consternation. Then arose a Babel of sounds: "Spy!" "Traitor!" "It is Hilda Fitzherbert"; "She must not leave the Hall alive"; "We have been betrayed." Shrieks and sobs were amongst the cries to be distinguished. Then there arose a mighty roar of "She must die," and a movement towards her. It was stilled for a moment. Lord Reginald rose, and, with a voice heard above all the rest, he thundered forth, "She shall not die. She shall live on one condition. Leave her to me"; and he strode towards her.

In one second the girl, like a fawn, sprang up the steps of the dais, and touched a button concealed in the wall, and then a second button. Words are insufficient to describe the effect.

The first button was connected with wires that ran through the flooring and communicated to every being in the Hall excepting to Hilda, on the insulated dais, a shock of magnetic electricity, the effect of which was to throw them into instantaneous motionless rigidity. No limb or muscle could be moved; as the shock found them they remained. And the pressure of the second button left no doubt of the fact, for it turned on the electric current to all the lamps inside and outside of the Hall, until the chamber became a blaze of dazzling light. There was no longer disguise of face or person, and every visage was at its worst. Fear, terror, cruelty, or revenge was the mastering expression on nearly every countenance. Some faces showed that the owners had been entrapped and betrayed into a situation they had not sought. But these were few, and could be easily read. On the majority of the countenances there was branded a mixture of greed, thwarted ambition, personal malignity, and cruelty horrible to observe. The pose of the persons lent a ludicrous aspect to the scene. Lord Reginald, for instance, had one foot in front of the other in the progress he was making towards Hilda. His body was bent forward. His face wore an expression of triumphant revenge and brutal love terrible to look at. Evidently he had thought there "was joy at last for my love and my revenge." Hilda shuddered as she glanced down upon the sardonic faces beneath her, and touched a third button. An answering clarionet at once struck out the signal to advance, and the measured tread of troops in all directions was heard. The poor wretches in the Hall preserved consciousness of what was passing around, though they could not exercise their muscular powers and felt no bodily pain. An officer at the door close to the dais saluted Miss Fitzherbert. "Be careful," she said, "to put your foot at once on the dais and come up to me." He approached her. "Have you your orders?" she asked.

"My orders," he said, "are to come from you. We have photographers at hand."

"Have a photograph," she instructed him, "taken of the whole scene, then of separate groups, and lastly of each individual. Have it done quickly," she added, "for the poor wretches suffer mental, if not physical, pain. Then everyone may go free excepting the occupants of the three top rows. The police should see that these do not leave Melbourne."

She bowed to the officer, and sprang down the steps and out of the Hall. At the outer door a tall form met her. She did not require to look—she was blinded by the light within—to be convinced that it was Colonel Laurient who received her and placed her in a carriage. She was overcome. The terrible scene she had passed through had been too much for her. She did not faint; she appeared to be in a state of numbed inertness, as if she had lost all mental and physical power. Colonel Laurient almost carried her into the house, and, with a face of deathly pallor, consigned her to the care of her sister. Maud had been partly prepared to expect that Hilda would be strongly agitated by some painful scene, and she was less struck by her momentary helplessness than by the agonised agitation of that usually self-commanding being Colonel Laurient. Probably no one had ever seen him like this before. It may be that he felt concern not only for Hilda herself, but for the part he had played in placing her in so agitating a position.

VII

Heroine Worship

It was nearly twelve o'clock before Hilda roused herself from a long and dreamless slumber, consequent upon the fatigue and excitement of the previous evening. She still felt somewhat exhausted, but no physician could have administered a remedy so efficacious as the one she found ready to hand. On the table beside her was a small packet sealed with the imperial arms. She removed the covering; and opening the case beneath, a beautifully painted portrait of the Emperor on an ivory medallion met her enraptured gaze. The portrait was set round with magnificent diamonds. But she scarcely noticed them; it was the painting itself that charmed her. The Emperor looked just as he appeared when he said to her, "Tell me now as woman to man, not as subject to emperor." There was the same winning smile, the same caressing yet commanding look. She involuntarily raised the medallion to her lips, and then blushed rosy red over face and shoulders. She turned the medallion, and on the back she found these words engraved: "Albert Edward to Hilda, in testimony of his admiration and gratitude." He must have had these words engraved during the night.

The maid entered. "Miss Fitzherbert," she said, "during the last two hours there have been hundreds of cards left for you. There is quite a continuous line of carriages coming to the door, and there have been bundles of telegrams. Miss Maud is opening them."

Hilda realised the meaning of the line—

"Do good by stealth, and blush to find it fame."

Then the maid told her Mrs. Hardinge was most anxious to see her and was waiting. She would not allow her to be awakened. Hilda said she would have her bath and see Mrs. Hardinge in the little boudoir adjoining her dressing-room in a few minutes.

Quite recovered from her last night's agitation, Hilda looked her best in a charmingly fashioned dressing-gown as she entered the room where Mrs. Hardinge was waiting to receive her.

"My dear, dear girl," said that lady as she embraced her, "I am delighted. You are well again? I need not ask. Your looks proclaim it. You are the heroine of the hour. The Emperor learnt everything last night, and the papers all over the world are full of it today. Maud says the telegrams are from every part of the globe, not only within our own empire, but from Europe, and the United States, and South America. You are a brave girl."

"Pray do not say so, Mrs. Hardinge. I only did my duty—what anyone in my place would have done. Tell me all that has happened."

Mrs. Hardinge, nothing reluctant, replied with animated looks and gestures. "Laurient has told me everything. You instructed the officer, it seems, to keep a watch over only the occupants of the three further rows. Lord Reginald had left those, and was approaching you. The officer, following your words literally, allowed him to leave unwatched. Some sixty only of the people were placed under espionage. Nearly everyone of the rest who were present is supposed to have left Melbourne, including Lord Reginald. We sent to his house to arrest him, but he had departed in one of his fastest long-distance air-cruisers. It is supposed that he has gone to Europe, or to America, or to one of his remote estates in the interior of this continent. I am not sure that the Emperor was displeased at his departure. When the intelligence reached him, he said to me, 'That will save Miss Fitzherbert from appearing in public to give evidence. As for the rest, it does not matter. They have been fooled to serve that man's ends.' So now they are free. But their names are known; indeed, their ridiculous appearance is immortalised. A likeness was taken of everyone, but the *tout ensemble* is superbly grotesque. It is well so few people know the secret of artificial magnetism."

Hilda showed Mrs. Hardinge the Emperor's magnificent present, and asked what was she to do. Should she write a letter of thanks?

"Do so," said the shrewd woman of the world. "Who knows that he will not value the acknowledgment as you value the gift?"

Again Hilda's face was suffused in red. "I must go away," she said to herself, "until I can better command myself." Then she begged Mrs. Hardinge not to mention about the Emperor's gift. "I shall only tell Maud of it. I felt it was right to tell you."

"Of course it was," said Mrs. Hardinge; "but it may be well not to mention it further. There are thousands of persons who honour and admire you; but there are thousands also who already envy you, and who will not envy you the less because of this great deed."

Then she told Hilda that the Emperor wished to do her public honour by making her a countess in her own right. Hilda shrank from the distinction. "It will lose me my seat in Parliament," she said.

"No. You will only have to stand for re-election, and no one will oppose you."

"But," said the girl, "I am not rich enough."

"If report is correct, you soon will be. The river-works in New Zealand are nearly finished; they will make you, it is said, a millionaire."

"I had forgotten them for the moment, but it is not safe to count on their success until the test is actually made. This reminds me that they will be finished next week; and my friends in New Zealand think that my sister and I ought to be present, if only in honour of our dear grandfather, who left us the interest we hold in the river. Can you spare me for ten days?"

"Of course I can, Hilda dear. The change will do you good. Laurient is going. He is said to have an interest in the works. And Montreal is going also. He too had an interest, but I think he parted with it."

They discussed whether Hilda should go to the fête that was to be held on Monday to celebrate the centenary of the completion of the irrigation of the Malee Scrub Plains.

These plains were once about as desolate and unromantic a locality as could be found; but a Canadian firm, Messrs. Chaffey Brothers, had undertaken to turn the wilderness into a garden by irrigation, and they had entirely succeeded. An enormous population now inhabited the redeemed lands, and a fête was to be held in commemoration of the century that had elapsed since the great work was completed. The Emperor himself had agreed to be there. Hilda begged to be excused. Her nerves were shaken. She would dread the many congratulations she would receive and the requests to repeat over and over again the particulars of the scene which inspired her now with only horror and repulsion.

"You must not show yourself today," Mrs. Hardinge said; "and I will cry you off tomorrow on the ground of illness. Next day go to New Zealand, and by the time you return you will be yourself again."

"You may say too I am abundantly occupied," said Hilda archly as Maud entered the room with an enormous package of open telegrams in her hands. "Dear Hilda, you do look well today. I am so pleased," said the delighted girl as she flung down the telegrams and embraced her sister. There was something singularly pathetic in the love of these two girls. Mrs. Hardinge left them together. Hilda showed the medallion in strict confidence. Maud was literally enraptured with it. "How noble, how handsome, he is! I know only one other man so beautiful." Then she paused in confusion; and Hilda rather doubted the exception, though she knew it was their old playfellow Montreal who was intended.

"Who is the traitor," she said, "you dare to compare with your Sovereign?"

Maud, almost in tears, declared she did not mean what she said. The Emperor was very handsome.

"Do not be ashamed, my dear, to be true to your feelings," said Hilda sententiously. "A woman's heart is an empire of itself, and he who rules over it may be well content with a single loyal subject."

"Nonsense, Hilda! Do not tease me. An emperor, too, may rule over a woman's heart."

This was rather carrying the war into the opposite camp. Miss Fitzherbert thought it time to change the subject. They discussed the telegrams. Then Maud told Hilda how frightfully agitated Laurient was the previous evening. Finally they decided they would go to New Zealand the day after the next. They debated if they should proceed in their own air-cruiser or in the public one that left early every morning. It was about a sixteen hours' journey in the public conveyance, but in their own it would take less time. Besides, they wished to go straight to Dunedin, where the girls had a beautiful residence, and where their friends were chiefly located. Hilda represented Dunedin in the New Zealand Parliament, and local government honours had been freely open to her; but, under the tutelage of Mrs. Hardinge, she had preferred entering into federal politics, though she continued in the New Zealand Parliament. Most of the leading federal statesmen interested themselves with one or other Dominion government. There was such an absence of friction between the federal and the separate dominion governments that no inconvenience resulted from the dual attention, while it led to a more intimate knowledge of local duties. Maud bashfully remembered that Lady Taieri had asked them to go to Dunedin on her beautiful cruiser. "She was making up a party," said Maud; "and she mentioned that Colonel Laurient and Lord Montreal were amongst the number."

Hilda saw the wistful look in Maud's eyes. "Let us go with Lady Taieri," she said; and so it was arranged.

VIII

AIR-CRUISERS

We trust our readers will not be wearied because it is necessary to give them at some length an explanation concerning the aerial machines to which reference has so often been made as air-cruisers. It need scarcely be said that from time immemorial a great deal of attention has been directed to the question whether aerial travelling could he made subservient to the purposes of man. Balloons, as they were called, made of strong fabrics filled with a gas lighter than air, were to some extent used, but rarely for practical purposes. They were in considerable request for military objects, and it is recorded that Gambetta managed to get out of Paris in a balloon when that city was beleaguered by the German army in 1871. The principle of the balloon was the use of a vessel which, weighing, with all its contents, less than a similar volume of the atmosphere, would consequently rise in the air. But evidently no great progress could be made with such an apparatus. The low specific gravity of the atmosphere forbade the hope of its being possible to carry a heavy weight in great quantity on a machine that depended for its buoyancy on a less specific gravity. Besides, there was danger in using a fabric because of its liability to irreparable destruction by the smallest puncture.

The question then was mooted, could not an aerial machine be devised to work although of higher specific gravity than the air? Birds, it was argued, kept themselves afloat by the motion of their wings, although their weight was considerably greater than a similar volume of the air through which they travelled. This idea was pursued. The cheap production of aluminium, a strong but light metal, gave an impulse to the experiment; and it was at length proved quite satisfactorily that aerial travelling was practicable in vessels considerably heavier than the air, by the use of quickly revolving fans working in the directions that were found to be suitable to the progress of the vessel. But great power was required to make the fans revolve, and the machinery to yield great power was proportionately heavy. It was especially heavy if applied separately to a portion of the fans, whilst it was dangerous to rely on one set of machinery, since any accident to it would mean cessation of the movement of the whole of the fans and consequently instant destruction. It was considered that, for safety's sake, there should be at least three sets of fans, worked by separate machinery, and that anyone set should be able to preserve sufficient buoyancy although the other two were disabled. But whilst it was easy to define the conditions of safety, it was not easy to give them effect. All applications of known engines, whether of steam, water gas, electricity, compressed air, or petroleum, were found to be too bulky; and although three sets of machines were considered necessary, one set only was generally used, and many accidents occurred in consequence. The aerial mode of travelling was much employed by the adventurous, but hundreds of people lost their lives annually.

At length that grand association the Inventors' Institution came to the rescue. The founders of the Inventors' Institution, though working really with the object of benefiting humanity, were much too wise to place the undertaking on a purely philanthropic basis. On the contrary, they constructed it on a commercial basis. The object was to encourage the progress of valuable inventions, and they were willing to lend sums from trifling amounts to very large ones to aid the development of any invention of which they approved. They might lend only a trifle to obtain a patent or a large sum to make exhaustive experiments. The borrower had to enter into a bond to repay the amount tenfold or to any less extent demanded by the Institution at its own discretion. It was clearly laid down that, when the invention proved a failure through no fault of the inventor, he would not be asked for any repayment. In case of moderate success, he would only be asked for moderate repayment, and so on. The fairness of the Institution's exercise of discretion was rarely, if ever, called into question. Once they lent nearly thirty thousand pounds to finally develop an invention. Within four years they called upon the inventor to repay nearly three hundred thousand, but he was nothing loath. The invention was a great commercial success and yielding him at the rate of nearly a million per annum. This association offered a large reward for the best suggestion as to the nature of an invention to render aerial travelling safe, quick, and economical. A remarkable paper gained the prize.

The writer was an eminent chemist. He expressed the opinion that the one possible means of success was the use of a power which, as in the case of explosives, could be easily produced from substances of comparative light weight. He urged, it was only of late years that any real knowledge of the nature of explosives was obtained. It was nearly four hundred years after the discovery of gunpowder before any possible substitutes were invented. It was again a long time before it was discovered that explosives partook of two distinctly separate characters. One was the quick or shattering compound producing instantaneous effect; the other was the slow or rending compound of more protracted action. He dwelt on the fact that in all cases the force yielded by explosives was through the change of a solid into a gaseous body, and that the volume of the gaseous body was greatly increased by the expansion consequent on the heat evolved during decomposition. The total amount of heat evolved during decomposition did not differ, but evidently the concentration of heat at anyone time depended on the rapidity of the decomposition. The volume of gas, independent of expansion by heat, varied also with different substances. Blasting oil, for instance, gave nearly thirteen hundred times its own volume of gas, and this was increased more than eight times by the concentration of heat; gunpowder only yielded in gas expanded by heat eight hundred times its own volume: or, in other words, the one yielded through decomposition thirteen times the volume of the other. He went on to argue that what was required was the leisurely chemical decomposition of a solid into a gas without sensible explosion, and of such a slow character as to avoid the production of great heat. He referred, as an example of the change resulting from the contact of two bodies, to the effect of safety matches. The match would only ignite by contact with a specially prepared surface. This match was as great an improvement on the old primitive match, as would be a decomposing material the force of which could be controlled, an improvement on the present means of obtaining power. He expressed a positive opinion that substances could be found whose rapidity of decomposition, and consequent heat and strength, could be nicely regulated, so that a force could be employed which would not be too sudden nor too strong to be used in substitution of steam or compressed air. He was, moreover, of opinion that, instead of the substances being mixed ready for use, with the concurrent danger, a mode could be devised of bringing the different component parts into contact in a not dissimilar manner to the application of the safety match, thereby assuring absolute immunity from danger in the carriage of the materials. This discovery could be made, he went on to say; and upon it depended improvement in aerial travelling. Each fan could be impelled by a separate machine of a light weight, worked with perfect safety by a cheap material; for the probabilities were, the substance would be cheaply producible. Each aerial vessel should carry three or four times the number of separate fans and machinery necessary to obtain buoyancy. The same substances probably could be used to procure buoyancy in the improbable event of all the machines breaking down. Supposing, as he suspected would be the case, that the resultant gas of the decomposition was lighter than air, a hollow case of a strong elastic fabric could be fastened to the whole of the outside exposed surface of the machine; and this could be rapidly inflated by the use of the same material. The movement of a button should be sufficient to produce decomposition, and as a consequence to charge the whole of this casing with gas lighter than the air. As the heat attending the decomposition subsided the elastic fabric would sufficiently collapse. The danger then would not be so much of descending too rapidly through the atmosphere as of remaining in it; a difficulty, however, which a system of valves would easily overcome.

The Institution offered twenty-five thousand pounds for a discovery on the lines indicated; and the Government offered seventy-five thousand pounds more on the condition that they should have the right to purchase the invention and preserve it as a secret, they supplying the material for civil purposes, but retaining absolute control over it for military purposes. This proviso was inserted because of the opinion of the writer that the effects he looked for might not so much depend on the chemical composition of the substances as on their molecular conditions, and that these might defy the efforts of analysts. If he was wrong, and the nature of the compound could be ascertained by analysis, the Government need not buy the invention; they could leave the discoverer to enjoy its advantages by patenting it, and share with other nations the uses that could be made of it for purposes of warfare.

It was sometime before the investigations were completely successful. There was no lack of attention to the subject, the inducements being so splendid. Many fatal accidents occurred through the widely spread attention given to the properties of explosives and to the possibility of modifying their effects. On one occasion it was thought that success was attained. Laboratory experiments were entirely satisfactory, and at length it was determined to have a grand trial of the substance. A large quantity was prepared, and it was applied to the production of power in various descriptions of machinery. Many distinguished people were present, including a Cabinet Minister, a Lord of the Admiralty, the

Under-Secretary for Defence, the President of the Inventors' Institution, several members of Parliament, a dozen or more distinguished men and women of science, and the inventor himself. The assemblage was a brilliant one; but, alas! not one of those present lived to record an opinion of the invention. The substance discovered was evidently not wanting in power. How far it was successful no one ever learnt. It may have been faultily made or injudiciously employed. But the very nature of the composition was lost, for the inventor went with the rest. An explosion occurred; and all the men and women within the building were scattered miles around, with fragments of the edifice itself. The largest recognisable human remains discovered were the well-defined joint of a little finger. A great commotion followed. The eminent chemist who wrote the paper suggesting the discovery was covered with obloquy. Suggestions were made that the law should restrain such investigations. Some people went so far as to describe them as diabolical. All things, however, come to those who wait; and at length a discovery was made faithfully resembling the one prognosticated by the great chemist.

Strange to say, the inventor or discoverer was a young Jewish woman not yet thirty years of age. From childhood she had taken an intense interest in the question, and the terrible accident above recorded seemed to spur her on to further exertion. She had a wonderful knowledge of ancient languages, and she searched for information concerning chemical secrets which she believed lost to the present day. She had a notion that the atomic structure of substances was better known to students in the early ages. It was said that the hint she acted on was conveyed to her by some passage in a Chaldean inscription of great antiquity. She neither admitted nor denied it. Perhaps the susceptibilities of an intensely Eastern nature led her to welcome the halo of romance cast over her discovery. Be that as it may, it is certain she discovered a substance, or rather substances which, brought into contact with each other, faithfully fulfilled all that the chemist had ventured to suggest. Together with unwavering efficiency there was perfect safety; and so much of the action depended on the structure, not the composition, that the efforts of thousands of *savants* failed to discover the secret of the invention. What the substances were in composition, and what they became after decomposition was easily determined, but how to make them in a form that fulfilled the purpose required defied every investigation.

The inventor did not patent her invention. After making an enormous fortune from it, she sold it to the Government, who took over the manufactory and its secrets; and whilst they sold it in quantity for ordinary use, they jealously guarded against its accumulation in foreign countries for possible warlike purposes. This invention, as much almost as its vast naval and military forces, gave to the empire of Britain the great power it possessed. The United States alone affected to underrate that power. It was the habit of Americans to declare that they did not believe in standing armies or fleets. If they wanted to fight, they could afford to spend any amount of treasure; and they could do more in the way of organising than any nation in the world. They were not going to spend money on keeping themselves in readiness for what might never happen. But we have not now to consider the aerial ships from their warlike point of view.

It should be mentioned that the inventor of this new form of power was the aunt of Colonel Laurient. She died nearly twenty years before this history, and left to him, her favourite nephew, so much of her gigantic fortune as the law permitted her to devise to one inheritor.

IX

TOO STRANGE NOT TO BE TRUE

A little after sunrise on a prematurely early spring morning at the end of August Lady Taieri's air-cruiser left Melbourne. There was sufficient heat to make the southerly course not too severe, and it was decided to call at Stewart's Island to examine its vast fishery establishments. A gay and happy party was on board. Lord and Lady Taieri were genial, lively people, and liked by a large circle of friends. They loved nothing better than to assemble around them pleasant companions, and to entertain them with profuse hospitality. No provision was wanting to amuse the party, which consisted, besides the two Miss Fitzherberts, Lord Montreal, and Colonel Laurient, of nearly twenty happy young people of both sexes. General and Lady Buller also were there. The General was the descendant of an old New Zealand family which had acquired immense wealth by turning to profitable use large areas of pumice-stone land previously supposed to be useless.

The Bullers were always scientifically disposed; and one lady of the family, a professor of agricultural science, was convinced that the pumice-stone land could be made productive. It was not wanting in fertilising properties; but the difficulty was that on account of its porous nature, it could not retain moisture. Professor Buller first had numerous artesian wells bored, and obtained at regular distances an ample supply of water over a quarter of a million of acres of pumice land, which she purchased for two shillings an acre. After a great many experiments, she devised a mixture of soil, clay, and fertilising agents capable of being held in water by suspension. She drenched the land with the water thus mixed. The pumice acted as a filter, retaining the particles and filtering the water. As the land dried it became less porous. Grass seed was surface-sown. Another irrigation of the charged water and a third, after some delay, of clear water, completed the work. When once vegetation commenced, there was no difficulty. The land was found particularly suitable for subtropical fruits and for grapes. Vast fruit-canning works were established; and a special effervescent wine known as Bullerite was produced, and was held in higher estimation than the best champagne. Whilst more exhilarating, it was less intoxicating. It fetched a very high price, for it could be produced nowhere but on redeemed pumice land. Not a little proud was General Buller of his ancestor's achievement. He was in the habit of declaring that he did not care for the wealth he inherited in consequence; it was the genius that devised and carried out the reclamation, he said, which was to him its greatest glory. Nevertheless in practice he did not seem to disregard the substantial results he enjoyed. General Buller was a soldier of great scientific attainments. His only child, Phoebe, a beautiful girl of seventeen, was with them. She was the object of admiration of most of the young men on board, Lord Montreal alone excepted. Beyond some conventional civilities, he seemed unconscious of the presence of anyone but Maud Fitzherbert; and she was nothing reluctant to receive his attentions.

The cruiser was beautifully constructed of pure aluminium. Everything conducive to the comfort of the passengers was provided. The machinery was very powerful, and the cruiser rose and fell with the grace and ease of a bird. After clearing the land, it kept at about a height of fifty feet above the sea, and, without any strain on the machinery, made easily a hundred miles an hour.

About four o'clock in the afternoon a descent was made on Stewart's Island. The fishing establishments here were of immense extent and value. They comprised not only huge factories for tinning the fresh fish caught on the banks to the south-east, but large establishments for dressing the seal-skins brought from the far south, as also for sorting and preparing for the market the stores of ivory brought from near the Antarctic Pole, the remnants of prehistoric animals which in the regions of eternal cold had been preserved intact for countless ages.

To New Zealand mainly belonged the credit of Antarctic research. Commenced in the interests of science, it soon became endowed with permanent activity on account of its commercial results. A large island, easily accessible, which received the name of Antarctica, was discovered within ten degrees of the Pole, stretching towards it, so that its southern point was not more than ten miles from the southern apex of the world. From causes satisfactorily explained by scientists, the temperature within a hundred-mile circle of the Pole was comparatively mild. There was no wind; and although the cold was severe, it was bearable, and in comparison with the near northern latitudes it was pleasant. On this island an extraordinary discovery was made. There were many thousands of a race of human beings whose existence was hitherto unsuspected.

The instincts of man for navigating the ocean are well known. A famous scientific authority, Sir Charles Lyell, once declared that, if all the world excepting one remote little island were left unpeopled, the people of that island would spread themselves in time over every portion of the earth's surface. The Antarctic Esquimaux were evidently of the same origin as the Kanaka race. They spoke a language curiously little different from the Maori dialect, although long centuries must have elapsed since the migrating Malays, carried to the south probably against their own will, found a resting-place in Antarctica. Nature had generously assimilated them to the wants of the climate. Their faces and bodies were covered with a thick growth of short curly hair, which, though it detracted from their beauty, greatly added to their comfort. They were a docile, peaceful, intelligent people. They loved to come up to Stewart's Island during the winter and to return before the summer made it too hot for them to exist, laden with the presents which were always showered upon them. They were too useful to the traders of Stewart's Island not to receive consideration at their hands. The seal-skins and the ivory obtained from Antarctica were the finest in the world, and the latter was procured in immense quantities from the ice-buried remains of animals long since extinct as a living race.

Lady Taieri's friends spent a most pleasant two hours on the island. Some recent arrivals from Antarctica were objects of great interest. A young chief especially entertained them by his description of the wonders of Antarctica and his unsophisticated admiration of the novelties around him. He appeared to be particularly impressed with Phoebe Buller. The poor girl blushed very much; and her companions were highly amused when the interpreter told them that the young chief said she would be very good-looking if her face was covered with hair, and that he would be willing to take her back with him to Antarctica. Lady Taieri proposed that they should all visit the island and be present at the wedding. This sally was too much. Phoebe Buller retired to her cabin on the cruiser, and was not seen again until the well-lighted farms and residences on the beautiful Taieri plains, beneath the flying vessel, reminded its occupants that they were close to their destination.

During the next six days Lady Taieri gave a series of magnificent entertainments. There were dances, dinner-parties, picnics, a visit to the glacier region of Mount Cook, and finally a ball in Dunedin of unsurpassed splendour. This was on the eve of the opening of the river-works; and all the authorities of Wellington, including the Governor and his Ministers, honoured the ball with their presence.

An account of the river-works will not be unacceptable. So long since as 1863 it was discovered that the river Molyneux, or Clutha as it was sometimes called, contained over a great length rich gold deposits. More or less considerable quantities of the precious metal were obtained from time to time when the river was unusually low. But at no time was much of the banks and parts adjacent thereto uncovered. Dredging was resorted to, and a great deal of gold obtained; but it was pointed out that the search in that manner was something like the proverbial exploration for a needle in a haystack. A great scientist, Sir Julius Von Haast, declared that during the glacial period the mountains adjacent to the valley of the Molyneux were ground down by the action of glaciers from an average height of several thousand feet. Every ounce of the pulverised matter must have passed through the valley drained by the river; and he made a calculation which showed that, if the stuff averaged a grain to the ton, there must be in the interstices of the river bed many thousands of tons of gold.

Nearly fifty years before the period of this history the grandfather of Hilda and Maud Fitzherbert set himself seriously to unravel the problem. His design was to deepen the bed of the Mataura river, running through Southland, and to make an outlet to it from Lake Whakatip. Simultaneously he proposed to close the outlet from the lake into the Molyneux and, by the aid of other channels, cut at different parts of the river to divert the tributary streams, to lay bare and clear from water fully fifty miles of the river bed between Lake Whakatip and the Dunstan. It was an enormous work. The cost alone of obtaining the various riparian and residential rights absorbed over two millions sterling. Twice, too, were the works on the point of completion, and twice were they destroyed by floods and storms.

Mr. Fitzherbert had to take several partners, and his own enormous fortune was nearly dissipated. He had lost his son and his son's wife when his grandchildren, Hilda and Maud, were of tender age. After his death the two girls found a letter from him in which he told them he had settled on each of them three thousand pounds a year and left to them jointly his house and garden near Dunedin, with the furniture, just as they had always lived in it. Beyond this comparatively inconsiderable bequest, he wrote, he had devoted everything to the completion of the great work of his life. It was certain now that the river would be uncovered; and if he was right in his expectations, they would become enormously wealthy. If it should prove he was wrong, "which," he continued, "I consider impossible, you will not think unkindly of the old grandfather whose dearest hope it was to make you the richest girls in the world." The time had come when these works, upon which so much energy had been expended, and which had been fruitful of so many disappointments, were to be finished; and a great deal of curiosity as to the result was felt in every part of the Empire. Hilda and Maud Fitzherbert had two and a half tenths each of the undertaking, and Montreal and his younger brother had each one tenth, which they had inherited, but it was understood that Montreal had parted with his own share to Colonel Laurient; two tenths were reserved for division amongst those people whose riparian and other rights Mr. Fitzherbert had originally purchased; and of the remaining tenth one half was the property of Sir Central Vincent Stout, Baronet, a young though very able lawyer, the other half belonged to Lord Larnach, one of the wealthiest private bankers in the Empire. There was by no means unanimity of opinion concerning the result of the works. Some people held, they would prove a total failure, and that the money spent on them had been wasted by visionary enthusiasts; others thought, a moderate amount of gold might be obtained; while very few shared the sanguine expectations which had led old Fitzherbert to complacently spend the huge sums he had devoted to his life's ideal. And now the result of fifty years of toil and anxiety was to be decided. It was an exceptionally fine day, and thousands of people from all parts of New Zealand thronged to the ceremony. Some preferred watching the river Molyneux subside as the waters gradually ran out; others considered the grander sight to be the filling of the new channel of the Mataura river.

It had been arranged that two small levers pressed by a child would respectively have the effect of opening the gates that barred the new channel to the Mataura and of closing the gates that admitted the lake waters to the Molyneux. As the levers were pressed a signal was to run down the two rivers, in response to which guns stationed at frequent intervals were to thunder out a salute.

Precisely at twelve the loud roar of artillery announced the transfer of the waters. Undoubtedly the grander sight was on the Mataura river. The progress of the liberated water as it rushed onward in a great seething, foaming, swirling mass, gleaming under the bright rays of the sun, formed a picture not easily to be forgotten. But the other river attracted more attention, for there not only nature played a part, but the last scene was to be enacted in a drama of great human interest. And this scene was more slowly progressing. The subsidence of the water was not very quick. The Molyneux was a quaint, many-featured river, partly fed by melted snow, partly by large surface drainage, both finding their way to the river through the lake, and by independent tributaries. At times the Molyneux was of great volume and swiftness. On the present occasion it was on moderate terms—neither at its slowest nor fastest. But as the river flowed on without its usual accession from the lake and the diverted tributaries, an idealist might have fancied that it was fading away through grief at the desertion of its allies. Lady Taieri's party were located on a dais erected on the banks of the river about twenty miles from the lake. After an hour or so the subsidence of the water became well marked; and occasionally heaps of crushed quartz, called tailings, from gold workings on the banks, became visible. Some natural impediments had prevented these from flowing down the river and built them up several feet in height. Here and there crevices, deep and narrow or shallow and wide, became apparent.

The time was approaching when it would be known if there was utter failure or entire success or something midway between. It had been arranged that, if any conspicuous deposit of gold became apparent, a signal should be given, in response to which all the guns along the river banks should be fired.

At a quarter past one o'clock the guns pealed forth; and loud as was the noise they made, it seemed trifling compared with the cheers which ran up and down the river from both banks from the throats of the countless thousands of spectators. The announcement of success occasioned almost delirious joy. It seemed as if every person in the vast crowd had an individual interest in the undertaking. The telephone soon announced that at a turn in the river about seven miles from the lake what appeared to be a large pool of fine gold was uncovered. Even as the news became circulated there appeared in the middle of the river right opposite Lady Taieri's stand a faint yellow glow beneath the water. Gradually it grew brighter and brighter, until at length to the eyes of the fascinated beholders there appeared a long, irregular fissure of about twenty-five feet in length by about six or seven in width which appeared to be filled with gold. Some of the company now rushed forward, and, amidst the deafening cheers of the onlookers, dug out into boxes which had been prepared for the purpose shovelsful of gold. Fresh boxes were sent for, but the gold appeared to be inexhaustible. Each box held five thousand ounces; and supposing the gold to be nearly pure, fifty boxes would represent the value of a million sterling.

Five hundred boxes were filled, and still the pool opposite Hilda was not emptied, and it was reported two equally rich receptacles were being drained in other parts. Guards of the Volunteer forces were told off to protect the gold until it could be placed in safety.

Hilda and Maud were high-minded, generous girls, with nothing of a sordid nature in their composition; but they were human, and what human being could be brought into contact with the evidence of the acquisition of such vast wealth without feelings of quickened, vivid emotion? It is only justice to them to say that their feelings were not in the nature of a sense of personal gratification so much as one of ecstatic pleasure at the visions of the enormous power for good which this wealth would place in their hands. Everyone crowded round with congratulations. As Colonel Laurient joined the throng Hilda said to him, "Why should I not equally congratulate you? You share the gold with us."

"Do I?" he said, with his inscrutable smile. "I had forgotten."

Lord Montreal, with a face in which every vestige of colour was wanting, gravely congratulated Hilda, then, turning to her sister, said in a voice the agitation of which he could not conceal, "No one, Miss Maud, more warmly congratulates you or more fervently wishes you happiness."

Before the astonished girl could reply he had left the scene. It may safely be said that Maud now bitterly regretted the success of the works. She understood that Montreal, a poor man, was too proud to owe to any woman enormous wealth. "What can I do with it? How can I get rid of it?" she wailed to Hilda, who in a moment took in the situation.

"Maud dearest," she said, "control yourself. All will be well." And she led her sister off the dais into the cruiser, in which they returned to Lady Taieri's house. They met Montreal in the gallery leading to their apartments. He bowed gravely.

Maud could not restrain herself. "You will kill me, Montreal," she said. "What do I care for wealth?"

"Maud, you would not have me sacrifice my self-respect," he said, and passed on.

He seemed almost unconscious where he was going. He was roused from his bitter reverie.

"Colonel Laurient will be greatly obliged if you will go to him at once," said a servant.

"Show me to his room," replied Montreal briefly.

"Laurient," said Montreal, "believe me, I am not jealous of your good fortune."

"My good fortune!" said Laurient. "I do not know of anything very good. I always felt sure that you would pay me what you owe me."

"Pay you what I owe you!" said Montreal, in a voice of amazement.

"Yes," replied Laurient. "You know that I come of a race of money-lenders, and I have sent for you to ask you for my money and interest."

But Montreal was too sad to understand a joke; and Laurient had noticed what passed with Maud, and formed a shrewd conjecture that the gold had not made either of them happy.

"Listen to me," he continued. "It is three years since you came to me and asked me to buy your share in the Molyneux works, as you had need of the money. I replied by asking what you wanted for your interest. You named a sum much below what I thought its value—a belief which today's results have proved to be correct. I am not in the habit of acquiring anything from a friend in distress at less than its proper value, and I was about to say so when I thought, 'I will lend this money on the security offered. I will not worry Montreal by letting him think that he is in debt and has to find the interest every half-year. There is quite sufficient margin for interest and principal too; and when the gold is struck, he will repay me.' I made this arrangement apparent in my will and by the execution of a deed of trust. The share is still yours, and out of the first money you receive you can repay me. Nay," he said, stopping Montreal's enthusiastic thanks. "I said I was a money-lender. Here is a memorandum of the interest, and you will see each year I have charged interest on the previous arrears—perfect usury. Go, my dear boy. I hate thanks, and I do not want money."

Montreal could not control himself to speak. Two minutes afterwards he was in Hilda and Maud's sitting-room. "Forgive me, Maud darling! I have the share. I thought I had lost it," he said incoherently; but he made his meaning clear by the unmistakable caress of a lover.

Hilda left the room—an example the historian must follow.

X

Lord Reginald Again

The following telegram reached Hilda next morning: "I heartily congratulate you, dear Hilda, on the success of your grandfather's great undertaking. The Emperor summoned me and desired me to send you his congratulations. I am also to say that he wishes as a remarkable event of his reign to show his approval of the patience, skill, and enterprise combined in the enormous works successfully concluded yesterday. The honour is to come to you as your grandfather's representative. Besides that, on account of your noble deed last week he wished to raise you to the peerage. He will now raise you to the rank of duchess, and suggests the title of Duchess of New Zealand; but that of course is as you wish. You must, my dear, accept it. A duchess cannot be an under-secretary, and I am not willing to lose you. Mr. Hazelmere has repeated his wish to resign; and I now beg you to enter the Cabinet as Lord President of the Board of Education, a position for which your acquirements peculiarly fit you. Your re-election to Parliament will be a mere ceremony. Make a speech to your constituents in Dunedin. Then take the waters at Rotomahana and Waiwera. In two months you can join us in London, where the next session of Parliament will be held. You will be quite recovered from all your fatigue by then."

In less than two weeks Hilda, Duchess of New Zealand, was re-elected to Parliament by her Dunedin constituents. Next day she left for Rotomahana with a numerous party of friends who were to be her guests. She had engaged the entire accommodation of one of the hotels.

Maud and Hilda before they left Dunedin placed at the disposal of the Mayor half a million sterling to be handed to a properly constituted trust for the purpose of encouraging mining pursuits, and developing mining undertakings.

New Zealand was celebrated for the wonderfully curative power of its waters. At Rotomahana, Te Aroha, and Waiwera in the North Island, and at Hammer Plains and several other localities in the Middle Island innumerable springs, hot and cold, existed, possessing a great variety of medicinal properties. There was scarcely a disease for which the waters of New Zealand did not possess either cure or alleviation. At one part of the colony or another these springs were in use the whole year round. People flocked to them from all quarters of the world. It was estimated that the year previous to the commencement of this history, more than a million people visited the various springs. Rotomahana, Te Aroha, and Waiwera were particularly pleasant during the months of October, November, and December. Hilda proposed passing nearly three weeks at each. Rotomahana was a city of hotels of all sizes and descriptions. Some were constructed to hold only a comparatively few guests and to entertain them on a scale of great magnificence. Every season these houses were occupied by distinguished visitors. Not infrequently crowned heads resorted to them for relief from the maladies from which even royalty is not exempt. Others of the hotels were of great size, capable indeed of accommodating several thousands of visitors. The Grandissimo Hotel comfortably entertained five thousand people. Most of the houses were built of ground volcanic scoria, pressed into bricks. Some of them were constructed of Oamaru stone, dressed with a peculiar compound that at the same time hardened and gave it the appearance of marble. The house that Hilda took appeared like a solid block of Carrara marble, relieved with huge glass windows and with balconies constructed of gilt aluminium. Balconies of plain or gilt aluminium adorned most of the hotels, and gave them a very pretty appearance. Te Aroha was a yet larger city than Rotomahana, as, besides its use as a health resort, it was the central town of an extensive and rich mining district. Waiwera was on a smaller scale, but in point of appearance the most attractive. Who indeed could do justice to thy charms, sweet Waiwera? A splendid beach of sand, upon which at short intervals two picturesque rivers debouched to the sea, surrounded with wooded heights of all degrees of altitude, and with many variations in the colour of the foliage, it is not to be wondered at that persons managed in this charming scene to forget the world and to reveal whatever of poetry lay dormant in their composition. Few who visited Waiwera did not sometimes realise the sentiment—

"I love not man the less, but nature more."

Hilda had duly passed through the Rotomahana and Te Aroha cures, and she had been a week at Waiwera, when one morning two hours after sunrise, as she returned from her bath, she was delighted at the receipt of the following letter, signed by Mrs. Hardinge:

"I have prepared a surprise for you, dearest Hilda. Mr. Decimus has lent me his yacht, and I am ready to receive you on board. Come off at once by yourself. We can talk over many things better here than on shore."

A beautifully appointed yacht lay in the offing six hundred yards from the shore, and a well-manned boat was waiting to take Hilda on board. She flew to her room, completed her toilet, and in ten minutes was on the boat and rowing off to the yacht. She ascended the companion ladder, and was received on deck by a young officer. "I am to ask your Grace to wait a few minutes," he said. Hilda gazed round the entrancing view on sea, land, and river, beaming beneath a bright and gorgeous sun, forgetting everything but the sense of the loveliness around her. She could never tell how long she was so absorbed. She aroused herself with a start to feel the vessel moving and to see before her the dreaded figure of Lord Reginald Paramatta.

Meanwhile the spectators on the shore were amazed to see Hilda go off to the yacht alone, and the vessel weigh anchor and steam away swiftly. Maud and Lady Taieri, returning from their baths along the beautiful avenue of trees, were speedily told of the occurrence, and a council rapidly held with Laurient and Montreal. Mrs. Hardinge's letter was found in Hilda's room.

"Probably," said Lady Taieri, "the morning is so fine that Mrs. Hardinge is taking the Duchess for a cruise while they talk together."

"I do not think so," said the Colonel. "Look at the speed the vessel is making. They would not proceed at such a rate if a pleasant sail were the only object. She is going at the rate of thirty miles an hour."

Maud started with surprise, and again glanced at the letter. "You are right, Colonel Laurient," she said, with fearful agitation; "this writing is like that of Mrs. Hardinge, but it is not hers. I know her writing too well not to be sure it is an imitation. Oh, help Hilda; do help her! Montreal, you must aid. She is the victim of a plot."

Meanwhile the vessel raced on; but with a powerful glass they could make out that there was only one female figure on board, and that a male figure stood beside her.

"Hilda," said Lord Reginald, bowing low, "forgive me. All is fair in love and war. My life without you is a misery."

"Do you think, my lord," said the girl, very pale but still courageous, "that this course you have adopted is one that will commend you to my liking?"

"I will teach you to love me. You cannot remain unresponsive to the intense affection I bear you."

"True love, Lord Reginald, is not steeped in selfishness; it has regard for the happiness of its object. Do you think you can make me happy by tearing me from my friends by an artifice like this?"

"I will make it up to you. I implore your forgiveness. Try to excuse me."

Hilda during this rapid dialogue did not lose her self-possession. She knew the fears of her friends on shore would soon be aroused. She wondered at her own want of suspicion. Time, she felt, was everything. When once doubt was aroused, pursuit in the powerful aerial cruiser they had on shore would be rapid.

"I entreat you, Lord Reginald," she said, "to turn back. Have pity on me. See how defenceless I am against such a conspiracy as this."

Lord Reginald was by nature brave, and the wretched cheat he was playing affected him more because of its cowardly nature than by reason of its outrageous turpitude. He was a slave to his passions and desires. He would have led a decently good life if all his wishes were capable of gratification, but there was no limit to the wickedness of which he might be guilty in the pursuit of desires he could not satisfy. He either was, or fancied himself to be, desperately in love with Hilda; and he believed, though without reason, that she had to some extent coquetted with him. Even in despite of reason and evidence to the contrary, he imagined she felt a prepossession in his favour, that an act of bravery like this might stir into love. He did not sufficiently understand woman. To his mind courage was the highest human quality, and he thought an exhibition of signal bravery even at the expense of the woman entrapped by it would find favour in her eyes. Hilda's words touched him keenly, though in some measure he thought they savoured of submission. "She is imploring now," he thought, "instead of commanding."

"Ask me," he said, in a tone of exceeding gentleness, "anything but to turn back. O Hilda, you can do with me what you like if you will only consent to command!"

"Leave me then," she replied, "for a time. Let me think over my dreadful position."

"I will leave you for a quarter of an hour, but do not say the position is dreadful."

He walked away, and the girl was left the solitary occupant of the deck. The beautiful landscape was still in sight. It seemed a mockery that all should appear the same as yesterday, and she in such dreadful misery. Smaller and smaller loomed the features on the shore as the wretched girl mused on. Suddenly a small object appeared to mount in the air.

"It is the cruiser," she exclaimed aloud, with delight. "They are in pursuit."

"No, Hilda," said Lord Reginald, who suddenly appeared at her side, "I do not think it is the cruiser; and if it be, it can render you no aid. Look round this vessel; you will observe guns at every degree of elevation. No cruiser can approach us without instant destruction."

"But you would not be guilty of such frightful wickedness. Lord Reginald, let me think better of you. Relent. Admit that you did not sufficiently reflect on what you were doing, and that you are ready to make the only reparation in your power."

"No," said Lord Reginald, much moved, "I cannot give you up. Ask me for anything but that. See! you are right; the cruiser is following us. It is going four miles to our one. Save the tragedy that must ensue. I have a clergyman in the cabin yonder. Marry me at once, and your friends shall come on board and congratulate you as Lady Paramatta."

"That I will never be. I would prefer to face death."

"Is it so bitter a lot?" said Lord Reginald, stung into irritation. "If persuasion is useless, I must insist. Come to the cabin with me at once."

"Dare you affect to command me?" said Hilda, drawing herself up with a dignity that was at once grave and pathetic.

"I will dare everything for you. It is useless," he said as she waved her handkerchief to the fast-approaching cruiser. "If it come too close, its doom is sealed. Be ready to fire," he roared out to the captain; and brief, stern words were passed from end to end of the vessel. "Now, Hilda, come. The scene is not one fit for you. Come you shall," he said, approaching her and placing his arm round her waist.

"Never! I would rather render my soul to God," exclaimed the brave, excited girl.

With one spring she stood on the rail of the bulwarks, and with another leapt far out into the ocean. Lord Reginald gazed on her in speechless horror, and was about to follow overboard.

"It is useless," the captain said, restraining him. "The boat will save her."

In two minutes it was lowered, but such was the way on the yacht that the girl floating on the water was already nearly a mile distant.

The cruiser and the boat raced to meet her. The yacht's head also was turned; and she rapidly approached the scene, firing at the cruiser as she did so. The latter reached Hilda first. Colonel Laurient jumped into the water, and caught hold of the girl. The beat was near enough for one of its occupants with a boathook to strike him a terrible blow on the arm. The disabled limb fell to his side, but he held her with iron strength with his other arm. The occupants of the cruiser dragged them both on board; and Colonel Laurient before he fainted away had just time to cry out, "Mount into the air, and fly as fast as you can." The scene that followed was tragical. Two of the occupants of the boat had grasped the sides of the cruiser, and were carried aloft with it. Before they could be dragged on board a shot from the yacht struck them both, and crushed in part of the side of the vessel, besides injuring many sets of fans. Another shot did damage on the opposite side. But still she rose, and to aid her buoyancy the casing was inflated. Soon she was out of reach of the yacht; and, with less speed than she left it, she returned to Waiwera. The yacht turned round, and steamed out to sea at full speed.

Hilda's immersion did her no harm, but her nerves were much shaken, and for many days she feared to be left alone. Colonel Laurient's arm was dreadfully shattered. The doctor at first proposed amputation, but the Colonel sternly rejected the suggestion. With considerable skill it was set, and in a few days the doctors announced that the limb was saved. Colonel Laurient, however, was very ill. For a time, indeed, even his life was in danger. He suffered from more than the wounded arm. Perhaps the anxiety during the dreadful pursuit as to what might be happening on board the yacht had something to do with it.

Hilda was untiring in her attention to Laurient; no sister could have nursed him more tenderly, and indeed it was as a sister she felt for him.

One afternoon, as he lay pale and weak, but convalescent, on a sofa by the window, gazing out at the sea, Hilda entered the room with a cup of soup and a glass of bullerite. "You must take this," she said.

"I will do anything you tell me," he replied, "if only in acknowledgment of your infinite kindness."

"Why should you talk of kindness?" said the girl, with tears in her eyes. "Can I ever repay you for what you have done?"

"Yes, Hilda, you could repay me; but indeed there is nothing to repay, for I suffered more than you did during that terrible time of uncertainty."

The girl looked very sad. The Colonel marked her countenance, and over his own there came a look of weariness and despair. But he was brave still, as he always was. "Hilda, dearest Hilda," he said, "I will not put a question to you that I know you cannot answer as I would wish; it would only pain you and stand in the way perhaps of the sisterly affection you bear for me. I am not one to say all or nothing. The sense of your presence is a consolation to me. No, I will not ask you. You know my heart, and I know yours. Your destiny will be a higher and happier one than that of the wife of a simple soldier."

"Hush!" she said. "Ambition has no place in my heart. Be always a brother to me. You can be to me no more." And she flew from the room.

XI

GRATEFUL IRELAND

At the end of October Maud was married from the house of the two sisters in Dunedin. No attribute of wealth and pomp was wanting to make the wedding a grand one. Both Maud and Montreal were general favourites, and the number and value of the presents they received were unprecedented. Hilda gave her sister a suite of diamonds and one of pearls, each of priceless value. One of the most gratifying gifts was from the Emperor; it was a small miniature on ivory of Hilda, beautifully set in a diamond bracelet. It was painted by a celebrated artist. The Emperor had specially requested the Duchess to sit for it immediately Maud's engagement became known. It was surmised that the artist had a commission to paint a copy as well as the original.

Immediately after the wedding Lord and Lady Montreal left in an air-cruiser to pass their honeymoon in Canada, and the Duchess of New Zealand at once proceeded to London, where she was rapturously received by Mrs. Hardinge. She reached London in time to be present at its greatest yearly fête, the Lord Mayor's Show, on the 9th November. According to old chronicles, there was a time when these annual shows were barbarous exhibitions of execrable taste, suitably accompanied with scenes of coarse vulgarity. All this had long since changed. The annual Lord Mayor's Show had become a real work of elaborated art. Either it was made to represent some particular event, some connected thread of history, or some classical author's works. For example, there had been a close and accurate representation of Queen Victoria's Jubilee procession, again a series of tableaux depicting the life of the virtuous though unhappy Mary Queen of Scots, a portrayal of Shakespeare's heroes and heroines, and a copy of the procession that celebrated the establishment of local government in Ireland. The present year was devoted to a representation of all the kings and queens of England up to the proclamation of the Empire. It began with the "British warrior queen," Boadicea, and ended with the grandfather of the present Emperor. Each monarch was represented with his or her retinue in the exact costumes of the respective periods. No expense was spared on these shows. They were generally monumental works of research and activity, and were in course of preparation for several years.

In many respects London still continued to be the greatest city of the Empire. Its population was certainly the largest, and no other place could compare with it in the possession of wealthy inhabitants. But wealth was unequally distributed. Although there were more people than elsewhere enjoying great riches, the aggregate possessions were not as large in proportion to the population as in other cities, such as Melbourne, Sydney, and Dublin. The Londoners were luxurious to the verge of effeminacy. A door left open, a draught at a theatre, were considered to seriously reflect on the moral character of the persons responsible for the same. A servant summarily dismissed for neglecting to close a door could not recover any arrears of wages due to him or her. Said a great lady once to an Australian gentleman, "Are not these easterly winds dreadful? I hope you have nothing of the kind in your charming country."

"We have colder winds than those you have from the east," he replied. "We have blasts direct from the South Pole, and we enjoy them. My lady, we would not be what we are," drawing himself up, "if the extremes of heat and cold were distasteful to us."

She looked at him with something of curiosity mixed with envy.

"You are right," she said. "It is a manly philosophy to endeavour to enjoy that which cannot be remedied."

The use of coal and gas having long since been abandoned in favour of heat and light from electricity, the buildings in London had lost their begrimed appearance, and the old dense fogs had disappeared. A city of magnificent buildings, almost a city of palaces, London might be termed. Where there used to be rookeries for the poor there were now splendid edifices of many stories, with constant self-acting elevators. It was the same with regard to residence as with food and clothing. The comforts of life were not denied to people of humble means.

Parliament was opened with much pomp and magnificence, and a mysterious allusion, in the speech from the throne, to large fiscal changes proposed, excited much attention. The Budget was delivered at an early date amidst intense excitement, which turned into unrestrained delight when its secrets were revealed. The Chancellor of the Exchequer, the Right Honourable Gladstone Churchill, examined critically the state of the finances, the enormous accumulations of the reserve funds all over the dominions, and the continued increase of income from the main sources of revenue. "The Government," he said, "are convinced the time has come to make material reductions in the taxation. They propose that the untaxable minimum of income shall be increased from five to six hundred pounds, and the untaxable minimum of succession value from ten to twelve thousand pounds, and that, instead of a fourth of the residue in each case reverting to the State, a fifth shall be substituted." Then he showed by figures and calculations that not only was the relief justifiable, but that further relief might be expected in the course of a few years. He only made one exception to the proposed reductions. Incomes derived from foreign loans and the capital value of such loans were still to be subject to the present taxation. Foreign loans, he said, were mischievous in more than one respect. They armed foreign nations, necessitating greater expense to the British Empire in consequence. They also created hybrid subjects of the Empire, with sympathies divided between their own country and foreign countries. There was room for the expenditure of incalculable millions on important works within the Empire, and those who preferred to place their means abroad must contribute in greater proportion to the cost of government at home. They had not, he declared, any prejudice against foreign countries. It was better for them and for Britain that each country should attend to its own interests and its own people. Probably no Budget had been received with so much acclamation since that in which the Chancellor of the Exchequer declared the policy of the Empire to be one of severe protection to the industries of its vast dominions.

Singularly, it was Lord Gladstone Churchill, great-grandfather of the present Chancellor of the Exchequer, who made the announcement, seventy years previously, that the time had arrived for abandoning the free trade which however he admitted had been of benefit to the parent country prior to federation.

The proposed fiscal reforms were rapidly confirmed; and Parliament rose towards the middle of December, in time to allow members to be present at the great annual fête in Dublin. We have already described how it was that the federation of the Empire, including local government in Ireland, was brought about by the intervention of the Colonies. The Irish people, warm-hearted and grateful, felt they could never be sufficiently thankful. They would not allow the declaration of the Empire to be so great an occasion of celebration, as the anniversary of the day on which the premiers of the six Australasian colonies, of the Dominion of Canada, and of the South African Dominion met and despatched the famous cablegram which, after destroying one administration, resulted in the federation of the empire of Britain. A magnificent group representing these prime ministers, moulded in life-size, was erected, and has always remained the most prominent object, in Dublin. The progress of Ireland after the establishment of the Empire was phenomenal, and it has since generally been regarded as the most prosperous country in the world. Under the vivifying influence of Protection, the manufactures of Ireland advanced with great strides. Provisions were made by which the evils of absenteeism were abated. Formerly enormous fortunes were drawn from Ireland by persons who never visited it. An Act was passed by which persons owning large estates but constantly absent from the country were compelled to dispose of their property at a full, or rather, it might be said, an excessive, value. The Government of Ireland declared that the cost of doing away with the evils of absenteeism was a secondary consideration. The population of Ireland became very large. Hundreds of thousands of persons descended from those who had gone to America from Ireland came to the country, bringing with them that practical genius for progress of all sorts which so distinguishes the American people. The improvement of Ireland was always in evidence to show the advantages of the federation of the Empire and of the policy of making the prosperity of its own people the first object of a nation.

The Irish fête-day that year was regarded with even more than the usual fervour, and that is saying a great deal. It was to be marked by a historical address which Mrs. Hardinge had consented to deliver. Mrs. Hardinge was the idol of the Irish. With the best blood of celebrated Celtic patriots in her veins, she never allowed cosmopolitan or national politics to make her forget that she was thoroughly Irish. She gloried in her country, and was credited with being better acquainted with its history and traditions than any other living being. She spoke in a large hall in Dublin to thousands of persons, who had no difficulty in hearing every note of the flexible, penetrating, musical voice they loved so well. She spoke of the long series of difficulties that had occurred before Ireland and England had hit upon a mode of living beneficial and happy to both, because the susceptibilities of the people of either country were no longer in conflict. "Undoubtedly," she said, "Ireland has benefited materially from the uses she has made of local government; but the historian would commit a great mistake who allowed it to be supposed that aspirations of a material and sordid kind have been at the root of the long struggle the Irish have made for self-government. I put it to you," she continued, amidst the intense enthusiasm of her hearers, "supposing we suffered from the utmost depression, instead of enjoying as we do so much prosperity, and we were to be offered as the price of relinquishing self-government every benefit that follows in the train of vast wealth, would we consent to the change?" The vehement "No" which she uttered in reply to her own question was re-echoed from thousands of throats. She directed particular attention to what she called the Parnell period. "Looked at from this distance," she said, "it was ludicrous in the extreme. Government succeeded Government; and each adopted whilst in office the same system of partial coercion, partial coaxing, which it condemned its successor for pursuing. The Irish contingent went from party to party as they thought each oscillated towards them. Many Irish members divided their time between Parliament and prison. The Governments of the day adopted the medium course: they would not repress the incipient revolution, and they would not yield to it. Agrarian outrages were committed by blind partisans and weak tools who thought that an exhibition of unscrupulous ferocity might aid the cause. The leaders of the Irish party were consequently placed on the horns of a dilemma. They had either to discredit their supporters, or to admit themselves favourable to criminal action. They were members of Parliament. They had to take the oath of allegiance. They did not dare to proclaim themselves incipient rebels." Then Mrs. Hardinge quoted, amidst demonstrative enthusiasm, Moore's celebrated lines—

> *"Rebellion, foul, dishonouring word,*
> *Whose wrongful blight so oft has stained*
> *The holiest cause that tongue or sword*
> *Of mortal ever lost or gained—*
> *How many a spirit born to bless*
> *Has shrunk beneath that withering name*
> *Whom but a day an hour's success,*
> *Had wafted to eternal fame."*

"But, my dear friends," pursued Mrs. Hardinge, "do not think that I excuse crime. The end does not justify the means. Even the harm from which good results is to be execrated. The saddest actors in history are those who by their own infamy benefited or hoped to benefit others.

"For one sad losel soils a name for aye,
However mighty in the olden time;
Not all that heralds rake from coffined clay,
Nor florid prose, nor honeyed words of rhyme
Can blazon evil deeds or consecrate a crime."

When the applause these lines elicited subsided, Mrs. Hardinge dilated on the proposed Home Rule that Mr. Gladstone offered. Naturally the Irish party accepted it, but a close consideration convinced her that it was fortunate it was not carried into effect. The local powers Mr. Gladstone offered were very moderate, far less than the Colonies then possessed, whilst, as the price of them, Ireland was asked to virtually relinquish all share in the government of the country. Gladstone saw insuperable difficulties in the way of establishing a federal parliament; and without it his proposals, if carried into operation, would have made Ireland still more governed from England than it was without the so-called Home Rule. In fact, the fruition of Mr. Gladstone's proposals would have driven Ireland to fight for independence. "We Irish are not disposed," declared Mrs. Hardinge, "to submit to be excluded from a share in the government of the nation to which we belong. Mr. Gladstone would virtually have so excluded us; and if we had taken as a boon the small instalment of self-government he offered, we could only have taken it with the determination to use the power we acquired for the purpose of seeking more or of gaining independence. Yes, my fellow-countrymen," she continued amidst loud cheers, "it was good for us, seeing how happily we now live with England, that we did not take Mr. Gladstone's half-measure. Yet there was great suffering and great delay. Weariness and concession stilled the question for a time; but the Irish continued in a state of more or less suppressed irritation, both from the sense of the indignity of not being permitted local government, and from the actual evils resulting from absenteeism. Relief came at length. It came from the great Colonies the energy of all of us—Irish, English, and Scotch—had built up." Long, continuous cheering interrupted the speaker. "You may well cheer," she continued. "The memory of the great colonial heroes whose action we this day commemorate, and whom, as usual, we will crown with wreaths of laurel, will always remain as green in our memory as the Isle of Erin itself." She proceeded to describe individually the prime ministers of the Colonies who had brought the pressure to bear upon the Central Government. "The Colonies," she said, "became everyday, as they advanced in wealth and progress, more interested in the nation to which they belonged. They saw that nation weakened and discredited at home and abroad by the ever-present contingency of Irish disaffection. They felt, besides, that the Colonies, which had grown not only materially, but socially, happy under the influence of free institutions, could not regard with indifference the denial of the same freedom to an important territory of the nation. Their action did equal honour to their intellect and virtue."

Mrs. Hardinge concluded by describing with inimitable grace the various benefits which had arisen from satisfying Ireland's wants. "The boon she received," the speaker declared, "Ireland has returned tenfold. It was owing to her that the Empire was federated; at one moment it stood in the balance whether this great cluster of States should be consolidated into the present happy and united Empire or become a number of disintegrated communities, threatened with all the woes to which weak States are subject."

After this address Mrs. Hardinge, in the presence of an immense multitude, placed a crown of laurel on the head of each of the statues of the colonial statesmen, commencing with the Prime Minister of Canada. Those statues later in the day were almost hidden from sight, for they were covered with a mass of many thousand garlands.

XII

THE EMPEROR PLANS A CAMPAIGN

One day early in May Colonel Laurient was alone with the Emperor, who was walking up and down the room in a state of great excitement. His eyes glittered with an expression of almost ferocity. The veins in his forehead stood out clear and defined, like cords. No one had seen him like this before. "To think they should dare to enter my territory! They shall never cease to regret it," he declared as he paced the room. Two hours before, the Emperor had been informed that the troops of the United States had crossed into Canada, the excuse, some dispute about the fisheries, the real cause, chagrin of the President at the Emperor's rejection of her daughter's hand.

"This shall be a bitter lesson to the Yankees," continued the Emperor. "They do not know with whom they have to deal. I grant they were right to seek independence, because the Government of my ancestor goaded them to it. But they shall learn there is a limit to their power, and that they are weak as water compared with the parent country they abandoned. Listen, Laurient," he went on more calmly as he took a seat by a table on which was spread a large map of the United States and Canada. "I have made up my mind what to do, and you are to help me. You are now my first military aide-de-camp. In that capacity and as head of the bodyguard you may appear in evidence."

"I shall only be too glad to render any assistance in my power. I suppose that the troops will at once proceed to Canada?"

"Would you have me," said the Emperor, "do such a wrong to my Canadian subjects? You know, by the constitution of the Empire, each State is bound to protect itself from invasion. Do you think that my Canadian volunteers are not able to perform this duty?"

"I know, your Majesty, that no finer body of troops is to be found in the Empire than the Canadian volunteers and Volunteer reserve. But I thought you seemed disinclined to refrain from action."

"There you are right, nor do I mean to remain idle. No; I intend a gigantic revenge. I will invade the States myself."

Colonel Laurient's eyes glittered. He recognised the splendid audacity of the idea, and he was not one to feel fear. "Carry the war into the enemy's camp!" he said. "I ought to have thought of it. It is an undertaking worthy of you, Sir."

"I have arranged everything with my advisers, who have given me, as commander of the forces, full executive discretion. You have a great deal to do. You will give, in strict confidence, to some person information which he is to cause to be published in the various papers. That information will be that all the ships and a large force are ordered immediately to the waters of the St. Lawrence. To give reality to the intelligence, the newspapers are to be severely blamed and threatened for publishing it. But you are to select trustworthy members of the bodyguard who are verbally to communicate to the admirals and captains what is really to be done. Nothing is to be put in writing beyond the evidence of your authority to give instructions, which I now hand to you. Those instructions are to be by word of mouth. All the large, powerful vessels on the West Indian, Mediterranean, and Channel stations are to meet at Sandy Hook, off New York, on the seventeenth evening from this, with the exception of twenty which are to proceed to Boston. They are to carry with them one hundred thousand of the Volunteer reserve force, fifty thousand of the regular troops, and fifty thousand ordinary volunteers who may choose to offer their services. In every case the ostensible destination is Quebec. My faithful volunteers will not object to the deceit. Part of the force may be carried in air-cruisers, of which there must be in attendance at least three hundred of the best in the service. The air-cruisers as soon as it is dark on the evening appointed are to range all round New York for miles and cut and destroy the telegraph wires in every direction. Twenty of the most powerful, carrying a strong force of men, are to proceed to Washington during the night and bring the President of the United States a prisoner to the flagship, the *British Empire*. They are to leave Washington without destroying property. About ten o'clock the men are to disembark at New York from the air-cruisers, and take possession of every public building and railway station. They are also during the night to disembark from the vessels. There will be little fighting. The Yankees boast of keeping no standing army. They have had a difficulty to get together the hundred and fifty thousand men they have marched into Canada. Similar action to that at New York is to be adopted at Boston. As soon as sufficient troops are disembarked I will march them into Canada at the rear of the invaders, and my Canadian forces are to attack them in front. I will either destroy the United States forces or take them prisoners. All means of transport by rail or river are to be seized, and also the newspaper offices. The morning publication of the newspapers in New York and Boston is to be suppressed; and if all be well managed, only a few New York and Boston people will know until late the day after our arrival that their cities are in my hands. My largest yacht, the *Victoria*, is to go to New York. I will join it there in an air-cruiser. Confidential information of all these plans is to be verbally communicated to the Governor of Canada by an aide-de-camp, who will proceed to Ottawa tomorrow morning in a swift air-cruiser. During this night you must arrange for all the information being distributed by trusty men. I wish the intended invasion to be kept a profound secret, excepting from those specially informed. Everyone is to suppose that Canada is the destination. I want the United States to strengthen its army in Canada to the utmost. As to its fleet, as soon as my vessels have disembarked the troops they can proceed to destroy or capture such of the United States vessels of war as have dared to intrude on our Canadian waters."

The Emperor paused. Colonel Laurient had taken in every instruction. His eyes sparkled with animation and rejoicing, but he did not venture to express his admiration. The Emperor disliked praise. "Laurient," he continued as he grasped his favourite's hand, "go. I will detain you no longer. I trust you as myself." The Colonel bowed low and hastened away.

It may seem that the proposed mobilization was incredible. But all the forces of the Empire were constantly trained to unexpected calls to arms. Formerly intended emergency measures were designed for weeks in advance; and though they purported to be secret, every intended particular was published in the newspapers. This was playing at soldiering. The Minister presiding over all the land and sea forces has long since become more practical. He orders for mobilization without notice or warning, and practice has secured extraordinarily rapid results.

XIII

Love and War

We seldom give to Hilda her title of Duchess of New Zealand, for she is endeared to us, not on account of her worldly successes, but because of her bright, lovable, unsullied womanly nature. She was dear to all who had the privilege of knowing her. The fascination she exercised was as powerful as it was unstudied. Her success in no degree changed her kindly, sympathetic nature. She always was, and always would be, unselfish and unexacting. She was staying with Mrs. Hardinge whilst the house she had purchased in London was being prepared for her. When Maud was married, she had taken Phoebe Buller for her principal private secretary. Miss Buller was devoted to Hilda, and showed herself to be a very able and industrious secretary. She had gained Hilda's confidence, and was entrusted with many offices requiring for their discharge both tact and judgment. She was much liked in London society, and was not averse to general admiration. She was slightly inclined to flirtation, but she excused this disposition to herself by the reflection that it was her duty to her chief to learn as much as she could from, and about everyone. She had a devoted admirer in Cecil Fielding, a very able barrister. As a rule, the most successful counsel were females. Men seldom had much chance with juries. But Cecil Fielding was an exception. Besides great logical powers, he possessed a voice of much variety of expression and of persuasive sympathy. But however successful he was with juries, he was less fortunate with Phoebe. That young lady did not respond to his affection. She inclined more to the military profession generally and to Captain Douglas Garstairs in particular. He was one of the bodyguard, and now that war was declared was next to Colonel Laurient the chief aide-de-camp. By the Colonel's directions, the morning after the interview with the Emperor, he waited on the Duchess of New Zealand to confer with her as to the selection of a woman to take charge of the ambulance corps to accompany the forces on the ostensible expedition to Canada. Hilda summoned Phoebe and told her to take Captain Garstairs to see Mary Maudesley, and ascertain if that able young woman would accept the position on so short a notice.

Hilda had always taken great interest in the organisation of all institutions dedicated to dealing with disease. Lately she had contributed large sums to several of these establishments in want of means, and she had specially endowed an ambulance institution to train persons to treat cases of emergency consequent on illness or accident. She had thus been brought into contact with Mary Maudesley, and had noticed her astonishing power of organisation and her tenderness for suffering. Mary Maudesley was the daughter of parents in humble life. She was about twenty-seven years of age. Her father was subforeman in a large metal factory. He had risen to the position by his assiduity, ability, and trustworthiness. He received good wages; but having a large family, he continued to live in the same humble condition as when he was one of the ordinary hands at the factory. He occupied a flat on the eighth story of a large residential building in Portman Square, which had once been an eminently fashionable neighbourhood. Besides the necessary sleeping accommodation, he had a sitting-room and kitchen. His residence might be considered the type of the accommodation to which the humblest labourers were accustomed. No one in the British Empire was satisfied with less than sufficient house accommodation, substantial though plain food, and convenient, decent attire.

Mary when little more than fourteen years old had been present at an accident by which a little child of six years old was knocked down and had one leg and both arms broken. The father of the child had recently lost his wife. He lived in the same building as the Maudesleys, and Mary day and night attended to the poor little sufferer until it regained health and strength. Probably this gave direction to the devotion which she subsequently showed to attendance on the sick. She joined an institution where nurses were trained to attend cases of illness in the homes of the humble. She was perfectly fearless, notwithstanding she had been twice stricken down with dangerous illness, the result of infection from patients she had nursed.

Miss Buller thought it desirable to see Miss Maudesley at her own house, both because it might be necessary to consult her further, and because she wished to observe what were her domestic surroundings. They were pleased with what they saw. The flat was simply but usefully furnished. There was no striving after display. Everything was substantial and good of its kind without being needlessly expensive. Grace and beauty were not wanting. Some excellent drawings and water-coloured paintings by Mr. Maudesley and one or two of his children decorated the walls. There were two or three small models of inventions of Mr. Maudesley's and one item of luxury in great beauty in the shape of flowers, with which the sitting-room was amply decorated. We are perhaps wrong in terming flowers luxuries, for after all, luxuries are things with which people can dispense; and there were few families who did not regard flowers as a necessary ornament of a home, however humble it and its surroundings might be.

Miss Buller explained to Miss Maudesley that the usual head of the war ambulance corps required a substitute, as she was unable to join the expedition. It was her wish as well as that of the Duchess of New Zealand that Miss Maudesley should take her place. Fortunately Miss Maudesley's engagements were sufficiently disposable to enable her to accept the notable distinction thus offered to her. Miss Buller was greatly pleased with the unaffected manner in which she expressed her thanks and her willingness to act.

Captain Garstairs returned with Phoebe Buller to her official room. "Goodbye, Miss Buller," he said. "I hope you will allow me to call on you when I return, if indeed the exigencies of war allow me to return."

"Of course you will return. And why do you call me Miss Buller?" said the girl, with downcast eyes and pale face. For the time all traces of coquetry were wanting.

"May I call you Phoebe? And do you wish me to return?"

"Why not? Goodbye."

The cold words were belied by the moistened eyes. The bold soldier saw his opportunity. Before he left the room they were engaged to be married.

It is curious how war brings incidents of this kind to a crisis. At the risk of wearying our readers with a monotony of events, another scene in the same mansion must be described.

The Emperor did Mrs. Hardinge the honour of visiting her at her own house. So little did she seem surprised, that it almost appeared she expected him. She, however, pleaded an urgent engagement, and asked permission to leave Hilda as her substitute. The readiness with which the permission was granted seemed also to be prearranged, and the astonished girl found herself alone with the Emperor before she had fully realised that he had come to see Mrs. Hardinge. He turned to her a bright and happy face, but his manner was signally deferential.

"You cannot realise, Duchess, how I have longed to see you alone once more."

Hilda, confused beyond expression, turned to him a face from which every trace of colour had departed.

"Do you remember," he proceeded, "the last time we were alone? You allowed me then to ask you a question as from man to woman. May I again do so?"

He took her silence for consent, and went on in a tone from which he vainly endeavoured to banish the agitation that overmastered him. "Hilda, from that time there has been but one woman in the world for me. My first, my only, love, will you be my wife?"

"Your Majesty," said the girl, who as his agitation increased appeared to recover some presence of mind, "what would the world say? The Emperor may not wed with a subject."

"Why not? Am I to be told that, with all the power that has come to me, I am to be less free to secure my own happiness than the humblest of my subjects? Hilda, I prefer you to the throne if the choice had to be made. But it has not. I will remain the Emperor in order to make you the Empress. But say you can love the man, not the monarch."

"I do not love the Emperor," said the girl, almost in a whisper.

These unflattering words seemed highly satisfactory to Albert Edward as he sought from her sweet lips a ratification of her love not for the Emperor, but the man.

They both thought Mrs. Hardinge's absence a very short one when she returned, and yet she had been away an hour.

"Dear Mrs. Hardinge," said the Emperor, with radiant face, "Hilda has consented to make me the happiest man in all my wide dominions."

Mrs. Hardinge caught Hilda in her arms, and embraced her with the affection of a mother. "Your Majesty," she said at length, "does Hilda great honour. Yet I am sure you will never regret it."

"Indeed I shall not," he replied, with signal promptitude. "And it is she who does me honour. When I return from America and announce my engagement, I will take care that I let the world think so."

On the evening which had been fixed, the war and transport vessels and air-cruisers met off New York; and in a few hours the city was in the hands of the Emperor's forces. There was a little desultory fighting as well as some casualties, but there were few compared with the magnitude of the operation. The railway and telegraph stations, public buildings, and newspaper offices were in the hands of the invaders. Colonel Laurient himself led the force to Washington. At about four o'clock in the morning between twenty and thirty air-cruisers, crowded with armed soldiers, reached that city. With a little fighting, the Treasury and Arsenal were taken possession of, and the newspaper offices occupied. About one thousand men invaded the White House, some entering by means of the air-cruisers through the roof and others forcing their way through the lower part of the palace. There was but little resistance; and within an hour the President of the United States, in response to Colonel Laurient's urgent demand, received him in one of the principal rooms. She was a fine, handsome woman of apparently about thirty-five years of age. Her daughter, a young lady of seventeen, was in attendance on her. They did not show much sign of the alarm to which they had been subjected or of the haste with which they had prepared themselves to meet the British envoy. They received Colonel Laurient with all the high-bred dignity they might have exhibited on a happier occasion. Throughout the interview his manner, though firm, was most deferential.

"Madam," he said, bowing low to the President, "my imperial master the Emperor of Britain, in response to what he considers your wanton invasion of British territory in his Canadian dominions, has taken possession of New York, and requires me to lead you a prisoner to the British flagship stationed off that city. I need scarcely say that personally the task so far as it is painful to you is not agreeable to me. I have ten thousand men with me and a large number of air-cruisers. I regret to have to ask you to leave immediately."

The President, deeply affected, asked if she might be allowed to take her daughter and personal attendants with her.

"Most certainly, Madam," replied Laurient. "I am only too happy to do anything to conduce to your personal comfort. You may be sure, you will suffer from no want of respect and attention."

Within an hour the President, her daughter, and attendants left Washington in Colonel Laurient's own air-cruiser. An hour afterwards a second cruiser followed with the ladies' luggage. Meanwhile the telegraph lines round Washington were destroyed, and the officers of the forces stationed at Washington were made prisoners of war and taken on board the cruisers. At six o'clock in the morning the whole of the remaining cruisers left, and rapidly made their way to New York. The President, Mrs. Washington-Lawrence, and her daughter were received on board the flagship with the utmost respect. The officers vied with each other in showing them attention, but they were not permitted to make any communication with the shore. About noon the squadron, after disembarking the land forces, left for the St. Lawrence waters, and succeeded in capturing twenty-five of the finest vessels belonging to the United States, besides innumerable smaller ones. The Emperor left fifty thousand men, well supplied with guns, arms, and ammunition, in charge of New York, and at the head of an army of one hundred thousand men, the flower of the British force in the Northern Hemisphere, proceeded rapidly to the Canadian frontier. About a hundred miles on the other side of the frontier they came upon traces of the near presence of the American forces.

Here it was that the most conspicuous act of personal courage was displayed, and the hero was Lord Reginald Paramatta. He happened to be in London when war was announced, and he volunteered to accompany one of the battalions. It should be mentioned that no proceedings had been initiated against Lord Reginald either for his presence at the treasonable meeting, or for his attempted abduction of Hilda. Her friends were entirely averse to any action being taken, as the publicity would have been most repugnant to her. It became necessary early in the night to ascertain the exact position of the American forces, and to communicate with the Canadian forces on the other side, with the view to joint action. The locality was too unknown and the night too dark to make the air-cruisers serviceable. The reconnoitring party were to make their way as best they could through the American lines, communicate with the Canadian commander, and return as soon as possible in an air-cruiser. Each man carried with him an electric battery of intense force, by means of which he could either produce a strong light, or under certain conditions a very powerful offensive and defensive weapon.

Only fifty men were to compose the force, and Lord Reginald's offer to lead them was heartily accepted. His bravery, judgment, and coolness in action were undeniable. At midnight he started, and, with the assistance of a guide, soon penetrated to an eminence from which the lights of the large United States camp below could be plainly discerned. The forces were camped on the plain skirted by the range of hills from one of which Lord Reginald made his observations. The plain was of peculiar shape, resembling nearly the figure that two long isosceles triangles joined at the base would represent. The force was in its greatest strength at the middle, and tapered down towards each end. Far away on the other edge of the plain, evidence of the Canadian camp could be dimly perceived. The ceaseless movements in the American camp betokened preparations for early action. After a long and critical survey both of the plain and of the range of hills, Lord Reginald determined to cross at the extreme left. The scouts of the Americans were stationed far up upon the chain of hills, and Lord Reginald saw that it would be impossible to traverse unnoticed the range from where he stood to the point at which he had determined to descend to the plain. He had to retire to the other side of the range and make his progress to the west (the camp faced the north) on the outer side of the range that skirted the camp. The hill from which he had decided to descend was nearly two miles distant from the point at which he made his observation. But the way was rough and tortuous, and it took nearly two hours to reach a comparatively low hill skirting the plain at the narrowest point. The force below was also narrowed out. Less than half a mile in depth seemed to be occupied by the American camp at this point. The Canadian camp was less extended. Its extreme west appeared to be attainable by a diagonal line of about two miles in length, with an inclination from the straight of about seventy degrees. Lord Reginald had thus to force his way through nearly half a mile of the camp, and then to cross nearly two miles between both forces.

The commander halted his followers, and in a low tone proceeded to give his instructions. The men were to march in file two deep, about six feet were to separate each rank, and the files were to be twenty feet apart. Each two men of the same file were to carry extended between them the flexible platinum aluminium electric wire, capable of bearing an enormous strain, that upon a touch of the button of the battery, carried by each man, would destroy any living thing which came in contact with it. Lord Reginald and the officer next to him in rank, who was none other than Captain Douglas Garstairs, were to lead the way. In a few moments the wires between each two men were adjusted. They were to proceed very slowly down the hill until they were observed, then with a rush, to skirt the outside of the camp. Once past the camp, the wires were to be disconnected, and the men, as much separated as possible, were to make to the opposite camp with the utmost expedition. Slowly and noiselessly amidst the intense shadow of the hill Lord Reginald and his companion led the way towards the extreme end of the camp. They had nearly reached the level ground when at three feet distance a sentry stood before them and shouted, "Who goes there?" Poor wretch, they were his last words. Lord Reginald and his companion with a rapid movement rushed on either side of him, and the moment the wire touched him he sank to the ground a lifeless mass. Then ensued a commotion almost impossible to describe. Lord Reginald and Captain Garstairs were noted runners. They proceeded at a strong pace outside of the tents. As the men rushed out to stop them, the fatal wire performed its ghastly execution. Three times three men sank lifeless in their path, before they cleared the outside of the tents. The Americans could only fire at intervals, for fear of hitting their own men. Of the twenty-five couples of Lord Reginald's force, fifteen passed the tents; twenty of the brave men were stricken down, whilst the way was strewn with the bodies of the Americans who had succumbed to the mysterious electric force. And now the time had come for each one to save himself. The wires were disconnected, the batteries thrown down, and for dear life everyone rushed towards the Canadian camp. But the noise had been heard along the line, and a wonderful consequence ensued. From end to end of the American camp the electric lights were turned on to the strength of many millions of candle-power. The lights left the camp in darkness; the rays were turned outwards to the spare ground that separated the camps. The Canadians responded by turning on their lights, and the plain between the two camps was irradiated with a dazzling brightness which even the sunlight could not emulate. The forlorn hope dashed on. Thousands of pieces were fired at the straggling men. It was fortunate they were so much apart, as it led to the same man being shot at many times. Of the thirty who passed the tents ten men at intervals fell before the murderous fire. Lord Reginald had been grazed by a shot the effects of which he scarcely felt. He and his companions were within a hundred yards of safety. But that safety was not to be. Captain Garstairs was struck. "Goodbye, Reginald. Tell Phoebe Buller—" He could say no more. Lord Reginald arrested his progress, and as coolly as if he were in a drawing-room lifted the wounded man tenderly and carefully in his arms, and without haste or fear covered the intervening distance to the Canadian camp. He was not struck. Who indeed shall say that he was aimed at? His great deed was equally seen by each army in the bright blaze of light; and when he reached the haven of safety, a cheer went up from each side, for there were brave men in both armies, ready to admire deeds of valour. Only ten men reached the Canadian camp; but, under the sanction of a flag of truce, five more were brought in alive, and they subsequently recovered from their wounds. Captain Garstairs was shot in the leg both above and below the knee. He remained in the Canadian camp that day.

At first it was feared he would lose the limb. But, to anticipate events, when the Emperor's forces joined the Canadian, Mary Maudesley took charge of him; and Captain Garstairs had ample cause to congratulate himself on the visit he had paid to secure the services of that lady. He was in the habit of declaring afterwards that it was the most successful expedition of his life, for it was the means of securing him a wife and of saving him a limb.

Lord Reginald rapidly explained the situation to the Canadian commander-in-chief. The Emperor's army could come up in three hours. It was evident from the movements under the hills opposite, as shown by the electric light, that the Americans did not mean to waste time. It was probable that at the first dawn of day they would set their army in motion; and it was arranged that the Canadians, without hastening the action, should, on the Americans advancing, proceed to meet them, so that they would be nearer the Emperor's forces as these advanced in rear of the enemy. Scarcely half an hour after he reached the Canadian lines Lord Reginald ascended in a swift air-cruiser, and passing high above the American camp, reached the Emperor's forces before day dawned.

Lord Reginald briefly communicated the result of his expedition. He took no credit to himself, did not dwell on the dangerous passage nor his heroic rescue of Captain Garstairs. Nevertheless the incident soon became known, and enhanced Lord Reginald's popularity.

The army was rapidly in motion; and after the Canadian and American forces became engaged, the British army, led by the Emperor in person, appeared on the crest of the hills and descended towards the plains. The American commander-in-chief knew nothing of the British army in his rear. Tidings had not reached him of the occupation of New York and Boston. The incident of the rush of Lord Reginald and his party across the plain from camp to camp and the return of an air-cruiser towards the United States frontier had occasioned him surprise; but his mind did not dwell on it in the midst of the immediate responsible duties he had to perform. On the other hand, he was expecting reinforcements from the States; and when the new force appeared on the summit of the hills, he congratulated himself mentally; for the battle with the Canadian army threatened to go hard with him. Before he was undeceived the British troops came thundering down the hills, and he was a prisoner to an officer of the Emperor's own staff. The British troops went onwards, and the destruction of the American forces was imminent. But the Emperor could not bear the idea of the carnage inflicted on persons speaking the same language, and whose forefathers were the subjects of his own ancestors. "Spare them," he appealed to the commander-in-chief. "They are hopelessly at our mercy. Let them surrender."

The battle was stayed as speedily as possible; and the British and Canadian forces found themselves in possession of over one hundred and thirty thousand prisoners, besides all the arms, ammunition, artillery, and camp equipage. It was a tremendous victory.

XIV

The Fourth of July Retrieved

The prisoners were left at Quebec suitably guarded; but the British and Canadian forces, as fast as the railways could carry them, returned to New York. The United States Constitution had not made provision for the imprisonment or abduction of the President of the Republic, and there was some doubt as to how the place of the chief of the executive should be supplied. It was decided that, as in the President's absence on ordinary occasions the deputy President represented him, so the same precedent should be followed in the case of the present extraordinary absence.

The President, however, was not anxious to resume her position. It was to her headstrong action that the invasion of Canada was owing. The President of the United States possesses more individual power in the way of moving armies and declaring war than any other monarch. This has always been the case. A warlike spirit is easily fostered in any nation. Still the wise and prudent were aghast at the President's hasty action on what seemed the slight provocation of the renewal of the immemorial fisheries dispute. Of course public opinion could not gauge the sense of wrong that the rejection by the Emperor of her daughter's hand had occasioned in the mind of the President. Now that the episode was over, and the empire of Britain had won a triumph which amply redeemed the humiliation of centuries back, when the English colonies of America won their independence by force of arms, public opinion was very bitter against the President. The glorious 4th of July was virtually abolished. How could they celebrate the independence and forget to commemorate the retrieval by their old mother-country of all her power and prestige? No wonder then that Mrs. Washington-Lawrence did not care to return to the States!

"My dear," she said to her daughter in one of the luxurious cabins assigned to them on the flagship, "do you think that I ought to send in my resignation?"

"I cannot judge," replied the young lady. "You appear quite out of it. Negotiations are said to be proceeding, but you are not consulted or even informed of what is going on."

"If it were not for you," said the elder lady, "I would never again set foot on the United States soil. Captain Hamilton" (alluding to the captain of the vessel they were on, the *British Empire*) "says I ought not to do so."

"I do not see that his advice matters," promptly answered the young lady. "If Admiral Benedict had said so, I might have considered it more important."

"I think more of the captain's opinion," said Mrs. Washington-Lawrence.

"Perhaps he thinks more of yours," retorted the unceremonious daughter. "But what do you mean about returning for my sake?"

"My dear, you are very young, and cannot remain by yourself. Besides, you will want to settle in the United States when you marry, to look after the large property your father left you, and that will come to you when you are twenty-one."

"I think, mother, you have interfered quite sufficiently about my marrying. We should not be here now but for your anxiety to dispose of me."

Mrs. Washington-Lawrence thought this very ungrateful, for her efforts were not at the time at all repugnant to the ambitious young lady. However, a quarrel was averted; and milder counsels prevailed. At length the elder lady confessed, with many blushes, Captain Hamilton had proposed to her, and that she would have accepted him but for the thought of her daughter's probable dissatisfaction.

This aroused an answering confession from Miss Washington-Lawrence. The admiral, it appeared, had twice proposed to her; and she had consented to his obtaining the Emperor's permission, a condition considered necessary under the peculiar circumstances.

The Emperor readily gave his consent. It was an answer to those of his own subjects who had wished him to marry the New England girl with the red hair, and opened the way to his announcing his marriage with Hilda.

The two weddings of mother and daughter took place amidst much rejoicing throughout the whole squadron. The Emperor gave to each bride a magnificent set of diamonds. Negotiations meanwhile with the United States proceeded as to the terms on which the Emperor would consent to peace, a month's truce having been declared in the meanwhile. Mrs. Hardinge and Hilda met the chief ministers of the two powerful empires in Europe, and satisfied them that the British Government would not ask anything prejudicial to their interests.

The terms were finally arranged. The United States were to pay the empire of Britain six hundred millions sterling and to salute the British flag. The Childrosse family and Rorgon, Mose and Co. undertook to find the money for the United States Government. The Emperor consented to retire from New York in six months unless within that time a plebiscite of that State and the New English States declared by a majority of two to one the desire of the people to again become the subjects of the British Empire, in which case New York would be constituted the capital of the Dominion of Canada. To anticipate events, it may at once be said that the majority in favour of reannexation was over four to one, and that the union was celebrated with enormous rejoicing. Most of the United States vessels were returned to her, and the British Government, on behalf of the Empire, voluntarily relinquished the money payment, in favour of its being handed to the States seceding from the Republic to join the Canadian Dominion. This provision was a wise one, for otherwise the new States of the Canadian Dominion would have been less wealthy than those they joined.

XV

CONCLUSION

The Emperor went to Quebec for a week, and thence returned to London, in the month of July. There he announced his intended marriage, and that it would very soon take place. The ovations showered on the Emperor in consequence of his successful operations in the United States defy description. He was recognised as the first military genius of the day. Many declared that he excelled all military heroes of the past, and that a better-devised and more ably carried-into-effect military movement was not to be found in the pages of history, ancient or modern.

At such a time, had the marriage been really unpopular, much would have been conceded to the desire to do honour to his military successes. But the marriage was not unpopular in a personal sense. There was great difference of opinion as to the wisdom of an emperor marrying a subject instead of seeking a foreign alliance. On the one hand, difficulties of court etiquette were alleged; on the other, it was contended that Britain had nothing to gain from foreign marriage alliances, that she was strong enough without them, and that they frequently were sources of weakness rather than strength.

The Duchess of New Zealand sat alone in her study in the new mansion in London of which she had just taken possession. It was magnificently furnished and decorated, but she would soon cease to have a use for it. She was to be married in a week, and the Empress of Britain would have royal residences in all parts of her wide dominions. She intended to make a present of her new house, with its contents, to Phoebe Buller on her marriage with Colonel Garstairs. He won his promotion in the United States war. She was writing a letter to her sister, Lady Montreal. A slight noise attracted her attention. She looked up, and with dismay beheld the face of Lord Reginald Paramatta. "How dare you thus intrude?" she said, in an accent of strong indignation, though she could scarcely restrain a feeling of pity, so ill and careworn did he look.

"Do not grudge me," he said, in deprecatory tones, "a few moments of your presence. I am dying for the want of you."

"My lord," replied Hilda, "you should be sensible that nothing could be more distasteful to me than such a visit after your past conduct."

"I do not deny your cause of complaint; but, Hilda—let me call you so this once—remember it was all for love of you."

"I cannot remember anything of the kind. True love seeks the happiness of the object it cherishes, not its misery."

"You once looked kindly on me."

"Lord Reginald, I never loved you, nor did I ever lead you to believe so. A deep and true instinct told me from the first that I could not be happy with you."

"You crush me with your cruel words," said Lord Reginald. "When I am away from you, I persuade myself that I have not sufficiently pleaded my cause; and then with irresistible force I long to see you."

"All your wishes," said the girl, "are irresistible because you have never learned to govern them. If you truly loved me, you would have the strength to sacrifice your love to the conviction that it would wreck my happiness." The girl paused. Then, with a look of impassioned sincerity, she went on, "Lord Reginald, let me appeal to your better nature. You are brave. No one more rejoiced than I did over your great deed in Canada. I forgot your late conduct, and thought only of our earlier friendship. Be brave now morally as well as physically. Renounce the feelings I cannot reciprocate; and when next I meet you, let me acknowledge in you the hero who has conquered himself."

"In vain. In vain. I cannot do it. There is no alternative for me but you or death. Hilda, I will not trifle with time. I am here to carry you away. You must be mine."

"Dare you threaten me," said she, "and in my own house?" Her hand was on the button on the table to summon assistance, but he arrested the movement and put his arm round her waist. With a loud and piercing scream, Hilda flew towards the door. Before she reached it, it opened; and there entered a tall man, with features almost indistinguishable from the profuse beard, whiskers, and moustache with which they were covered. Hilda screamed out, "Help me. Protect me."

"I am Laurient," he whispered to the agitated girl. "Go to the back room, and this whistle will bring immediate aid. The lower part of the house and staircase are crowded with that man's followers." Hilda rushed from the room before Lord Reginald could reach her. Colonel Laurient closed the door, and pulled from his face its hirsute adornments. "I am

Colonel Laurient, at your service. You have to reckon with me for your cruel persecution of that poor girl."

"How came you here?" asked Lord Reginald, who was almost stunned with astonishment.

"My lord," replied Laurient, "since your attempt at Waiwera to carry the Duchess away you have been unceasingly shadowed. Your personal attendants were in the pay of those who watched over that fair girl's safety. Your departure from Canada was noted, the object of your stay in London suspected. Your intended visit today was guessed at, and I was one of the followers who accompanied you. But there is no time for explanation. You shall account to me as a friend of the Emperor for your conduct to the noble woman he is about to marry. She shall be persecuted no longer; one or both of us shall not leave this room alive."

He pulled out two small firing-pieces, each with three barrels. "Select one," he said briefly. "Both weapons are loaded. We shall stand at opposite ends of this large room."

At no time would Lord Reginald have been likely to refuse a challenge of this kind, and least of all now. His one desire was revenge on someone to satisfy the terrible cravings of his baffled passions. "I am under the impression," he said, with studied calmness, "that I already owe something to your interference. I am not reluctant to acquit myself of the debt."

In a few minutes the help Hilda summoned arrived. Laurient had taken care to provide assistance near at hand. When the officers in charge of the aid entered the room, a sad sight presented itself. Both Lord Reginald and Colonel Laurient were prostrate on the ground, the former evidently fatally stricken, the latter scarcely less seriously wounded.

They did not venture to move Lord Reginald. At his earnest entreaty, Hilda came to him. It was a terrible ordeal for her. It was likely both men would die, and their death would be the consequence of their vain love for her. But how different the nature of the love, the one unselfish and sacrificing, seeking only her happiness, the other brutally indifferent to all but its own uncontrollable impulses. It seemed absurd to call by the same name sentiments so widely opposite, the one so ennobling, the other so debasing.

She stood beside the couch on which they had lifted him. "Hilda," he whispered in a tone so low, she could scarcely distinguish what he said, "the death I spoke of has come; and I do not regret it. It was you or death, as I told you; and death has conquered." He paused for a few moments, then resumed, "My time is short. Say you forgive me all the unhappiness I have caused you."

Hilda was much affected. "Reginald," she faltered, "I fully, freely forgive you for all your wrongs to me; but can I forget that Colonel Laurient may also meet his death?"

"A happy death, for it will have been gained in your service."

"Reginald, dear Reginald, if your sad anticipation is to be realised, should you not cease to think of earthly things?"

"Pray for me," he eagerly replied. "You were right in saying my passions were ungovernable, but I have never forgotten the faith of my childhood. I am past forgiveness, for I sinned and knew that I was sinning."

"God is all-merciful," said the tearful girl. She sank upon her knees before the couch, and in low tones prayed the prayers familiar to her, and something besides extemporised from her own heart. She thought of Reginald as she first knew him, of the great deeds of which he had been capable, of the melancholy consequence of his uncontrolled love for herself. She prayed with an intense earnestness that he might be forgiven; and as she prayed a faint smile irradiated the face of the dying man, and with an effort to say, "Amen," he drew his last breath.

Three days later Hilda stood beside another deathbed. All that care and science could effect was useless; Colonel Laurient was dying. The fiat had gone forth; life was impossible. The black horses would once more come to the door of the new mansion. He who loved Hilda so truly, so unselfishly, was to share the fate of that other unworthy lover. Hilda's grief was of extreme poignancy, and scarcely less grieved was the Emperor himself. He had passed most of his time since he had learnt Laurient's danger beside his couch, and now the end was approaching. On one side of the bed was the Emperor, on the other Hilda, Duchess of New Zealand. How puerile the title seemed in the presence of the dread executioner who recognises no distinction between peasant and monarch. The mightiest man on earth was utterly powerless to save his friend, and the day would come when he and the lovely girl who was to be his bride would be equally powerless to prolong their own lives. In such a presence the distinctions of earth seemed narrowed and distorted.

"Sir," said the dying man, "my last prayer is that you and Hilda may be happy. She is the noblest woman I have ever met. You once told me," he said, turning to her, "that you felt for me a sister's love. Will you before I die give me a sister's kiss and blessing?" Hilda, utterly unable to control her sobs, bent down and pressed a kiss upon his lips. It seemed as if life passed away at that very moment. He never moved or spoke again. He was buried in the grounds of one of the royal residences, and the Emperor and Hilda erected a splendid monument to his memory. No year ever passed without their visiting the grave of the man who had served them so well.

Their marriage was deferred for a month in consequence of Colonel Laurient's death, but the ceremony was a grand one. Nothing was wanting in the way of pomp and display to invest it with the utmost importance. Throughout the whole Empire there were great rejoicings. It really appeared as if the Emperor could not have made a more popular marriage, and that unalloyed happiness was in store for him and his bride.

Epilogue

Twenty years have passed. The Emperor is nearly fifty, and the Empress is no longer young. They have preserved their good looks; but on the countenance of each is a settled melancholy expression, wanting in the days which preceded their marriage. Their union seemed to promise a happy life, no cloud showed itself on the horizon of their new existence, and yet sadness proved to be its prominent feature. A year after their marriage a son was born, amidst extravagant rejoicings throughout the Empire. Another year witnessed the birth of a daughter, and a third child was shortly expected, when a terrible event occurred. A small dog, a great favourite of the child, slightly bit the young prince. The animal proved to be mad, a fact unsuspected until too late to apply adequate remedial measures to the boy, and the heir to the Empire died amidst horrible suffering. The grief of the parents may be better imagined than described. The third child, a boy, was prematurely born, and grew up weak and sickly. Two more children were subsequently born, but both died in early childhood. The princess, the elder-born of the two survivors, grew into a beautiful woman. She was over eighteen years old when this history reopens. Her brother was a year younger. The contrast between the two was remarkable. Princess Victoria was a fine, healthy girl, with a lovely complexion. She inherited her mother's beauty and her father's dignity and grace of manner. She was the idol of everyone with whom she came in contact. The charm and fascination of her demeanour were enhanced by the dignity of presence which never forsook her. Her brother, poor boy, was thin and delicate-looking, and a constant invalid, though not afflicted with any organic disease. They both were clever, but their tastes were widely apart. The Princess was an accomplished linguist; and few excelled her in knowledge of history, past and contemporaneous. She took great interest in public affairs. No statesman was better acquainted with the innumerable conditions which cumbered the outward seeming of affairs of state. Prince Albert Edward, on the contrary, took no heed of public affairs. He rarely read a newspaper; but he was a profound mathematician, a constant student of physical laws: and, above all, he had a love for the study of human character. When only sixteen, he gained a gold medal for a paper sent in anonymously to the Imperial Institute, dealing with the influence of circumstances and events upon mental and moral development.

The essay was very deep, and embodied some new and rather startling theories, closely reasoned, as to the effects of training and education.

The Princess was her father's idol; and though he was too just to wish to prejudice his son's rights, he could not without bitter regret remember that but for his action long ago his daughter would have been heiress to the throne. Fate, with strange irony, had made the Empress also alter her views. The weak and sickly son had been the special object of long years of care. The poor mother, bereaved of three children out of five, clung to this weak offspring as the shipwrecked sailor to the plank which is his sole chance of life. The very notion of the loved son losing the succession was a cruel shock to her. The theoretical views which she shared with Mrs. Hardinge years since, were a weak barrier to the promptings of maternal love.

So it happened that the Emperor ardently regretted that he had prevented the proposed change in the order of succession, and the Empress as much rejoiced that the views of her party had not prevailed. But the Emperor was essentially a just man. He recognised that before children had been born to him the question was open to treatment, but that it was different now when his son enjoyed personal rights. Ardently as he desired his daughter should reign, he would not on any consideration agree that his son should be set aside without his own free and full consent. What annoyed him most was the fallacy of his own arguments long ago. It will be remembered, he had laid chief stress on the probability that the female succession would reduce the chance of the armies being led by the Emperor in person in case of war. But it was certain that, if his son succeeded, he would not head the army in battle. The young Prince had passed through the military training prescribed for every male subject of the Empire, but he had no taste for military knowledge. Not that he wanted courage; on the contrary, he had displayed conspicuous bravery on several occasions. Once he had jumped off a yacht in rough weather to save one of his staff who had fallen overboard; and on another occasion, when a fire took place at sea, he was cooler and less terror-stricken than any of the persons who surrounded him. But for objects and studies of a militant character he had an aversion, almost a contempt; and it was certain he never would become a great general. The fallacy of his principal objection to the change in the order of succession was thus brought home to the Emperor with bitter emphasis.

Perhaps the worst effect of all was the wall of estrangement that was being built up between him and the Empress. When two people constantly in communication feel themselves prevented from discussing the subject nearest to the heart and most constant to the mind of each, estrangement must grow up, no matter how great may be their mutual love. The Emperor and Empress loved each other as much as ever, but to both the discussion of the question of succession was fraught with bitter pain.

The time had, however, come when they must discuss it. The Princess had already reached her legal majority, and the Prince would shortly arrive at the age which was prescribed as the majority of the heir to the throne. His own unfitness for the sovereignty and the exceeding suitability of his sister were widely known, and the newspapers had just commenced a warm discussion on the subject. The Cabinet, too, were inclined to take action. Many years since, Mrs. Hardinge died quite suddenly of heart disease; and Lady Cairo had for a long period filled the post of Prime Minister. Lady Garstairs, *née* Phoebe Buller, was leader of the Opposition. She was still a close friend of the Empress, and she shared the opinion of her imperial mistress that the subject had better not be dealt with. But Lady Cairo, who had always thought it ought to have been settled before the Emperor's marriage, was very much embarrassed now by the strong and general demand that the question should be immediately reopened. She had several interviews with the Emperor on the subject. His Majesty did not conceal his personal desire that his daughter should succeed, or his opinion that she was signally fitted for the position; but nothing, he declared, would induce him to allow his son's rights to be assailed without the Prince's full and free consent. Meanwhile the Prince showed no sign. It seemed as if he alone of all the subjects of the Empire knew and cared nothing about the matter. He rarely spoke of public affairs, and scarcely ever read the newspapers, especially those portions of them devoted to politics.

The Emperor felt a discussion with the Empress could no longer be avoided; and we meet them once more at a long and painful interview, in which they unburdened the thoughts which each had concealed from the other for years past.

"Dear Hilda," said the Emperor, "do not misunderstand me. I would rather renounce the crown than allow our son's rights to be prejudiced without his approval."

"Yes, yes, I understand that," said the Empress; "and I recognise your sense of justice. I do not think that you love Albert as much as you do Victoria, and you certainly have not that pride in him which you have in her; whilst I—I love my boy, and cannot bear that he should suffer."

"My dear," said the Emperor, "that is where we differ. I love Albert, and I admire his high character; but I do not think it would be for his happiness that he should reign, nor that he should now relinquish all the studies in which he delights, in order to take his proper position as heir to the throne. In a few weeks he will be of age; and if he is to succeed me, duties of a most onerous and constant character will devolve on him. He is, I will do him the justice to say, too conscientious to neglect his duty; and I believe he will endeavour to attend to public affairs and cast away all those studies that most delight him: but the change will make him miserable."

"You are a wise judge of the hearts and ways of men and women, and it would ill become me to disregard your opinion; but, Albert, does it not occur to you that our Albert might live to regret any renunciation he made in earlier life?"

"I admit the possibility," said the Emperor; "but he is stable and mature beyond his years. His dream is to benefit mankind by the studies he pursues. He has already met with great success in those studies, and I think they will bring their own reward; but should anything occur to make him renounce them, he may, I admit, lament too late the might-have-been."

"Supposing," said the Empress, "he married an ambitious wife and had sons like you were, dear Albert, in your young manhood?"

"One cannot judge one's self; yet I think I should have accepted whatever was my position, and not have allowed vain repinings to prevent my endeavouring to perform the duties that devolved on me."

"Forgive me, Albert, for doubting it. You would, I am sure, have been true to yourself."

"You confirm my own impression. Recollect, Hilda, true ambition prompts to legitimate effort, not to vain grief for the unattainable. It may be that Victoria's own children will succeed; but Albert's children, if they are ambitious, will not be denied a brilliant career."

"I cannot argue the matter, for it is useless to deny that I refuse to see our son as he is. I love him to devotion, yet the grief is always with me that the son is not like the father."

"Hilda dear, he is not like the father in some respects; but the very difference perhaps partakes of the higher life. When the last day comes to him and to me, who shall say that he will not look back to his conduct through life with more satisfaction than I shall be able to do?"

"I will not allow you to underrate yourself. You are faultless in my eyes. No human being has ever had cause to complain of you."

"Tut! tut! You are too partial a judge." But he kissed her tenderly, and his eyes gleamed with a pleasure for a very long while unknown to them, as she brought to him the conviction that the love and admiration of her youth had survived all the sorrows of their after-lives.

At this juncture the Prince entered the room. "Pardon me," he said. "I thought my mother was alone"; and he was about to retire. The Emperor looked at the Empress, and he gathered from her answering glance that she shared with him the desire that all reserve and concealment should be at an end. In a moment his resolution was formed. His son should know everything and decide for himself.

"Stay, Albert," he said. "I am glad to have an opportunity of talking with you in the presence of your mother."

"I am equally glad, Sir. Indeed, I should have asked you later in the day to have given me an audience."

"Why do you wish to see me?" said the Emperor, who in a moment suspected what proved to be the case: that his son anticipated his own wish for an exchange of confidence.

"During the last few days it has become known to me, Sir, that a controversy is going on respecting the order of succession to the throne. I have," producing a small package, "cuttings from some of the principal newspapers from which I gather there is a strong opinion in favour of a change in the order of succession. I glean from them that by far the larger number are agreed on the point that it would be better my sister should succeed to you." He paused a moment, and then in a clear and distinct tone said, "I am of the same opinion."

The Empress interposed. "Are you sure of your own mind? Do you recognise what it is you would renounce—the position of foremost ruler on the wide globe?"

"I think I realise it. I am not much given to the study of contemporaneous history, but I am well acquainted with all the circumstances of my father's great career." The parents looked at each other in surprise. "Yes; there is no one," he resumed, "who is more proud of the Emperor than his only son."

With much emotion the father clasped the son's hand. "What is it you wish, Albert?" he said.

"I would like Victoria to be present if you would not mind," replied the Prince, looking at his mother. "May I fetch her?"

The Empress nodded. "You will find her in the next room."

The Princess Victoria was a lovely and splendid girl. It was impossible to look at her without feeling that she would adorn the highest position. The Emperor's face lighted up as he glanced at her; and the Empress, much impressed with what her husband had said, kissed the Princess with unusual tenderness. She probably wished her daughter to feel that she was not averse to any issue which might result from the momentous interview about to take place.

"Sir," said the young Prince, addressing his father, "I know how important your time is, so I will not prolong what I wish to say. Until I saw these papers," holding up the extracts, "I confess I was unaware of the great interest which is now being taken in the question of the succession. But I cannot assert that the subject is new to me; on the contrary, I have thought it over deeply, and it was my intention to speak to you about it when in a few weeks I should attain my majority."

"My dear boy, pray believe that it was through consideration to you I have refrained from speaking to you on the subject."

"I know it, Sir, and thank you," said the boy with feeling; "but the time has come when there must be no longer any reserve between us. You know, I do not take much interest in public affairs, and I fear it has grieved you that my inclinations have been so alien to what my position as heir to the throne required. But I am not unacquainted with the principles of the constitution of the Empire. I will not pretend that I have studied them from a statesman's point of view. They have absorbed my attention in the course of my favourite study of human character. I have closely (if it did not seem conceited, I might say philosophically) investigated the Constitution with the object of determining to what extent it operates as an educational medium affecting the character of the nation. The question of the succession is settled by the Constitution Act, and no alteration is possible in justice, that does not fully reserve the rights of all living beings. I am first in the order of succession, and no law of man can take it from me excepting with my full consent."

"Albert," interrupted the Emperor, "you say rightly; and I assure you that I am fully prepared to adopt this view. No consideration will induce me to consent to any alteration which will prejudice you excepting with your own desire; and indeed I am doubtful if even with your desire I should be justified in allowing you at so early a period of your life to make a renunciation."

"I am grateful, Sir, for this assurance. Its memory will live in my mind. And now let me say that, having for a long while considered the subject with the utmost attention I could give to it, I am of opinion that the present law by which the female succession is partly barred is not a just one. I will not, however, say that it ought to be altered against a living representative; but I decidedly think that it should be amended as regards those unborn. The decision I have come to then does not depend upon the amendment in the Constitution which I believe to be desirable. It arises from personal causes. I believe that my sister Victoria is as specially fitted for the dignity and functions of empress, as I am the reverse."

The Princess Victoria started up in great agitation. She was not without ambition, and it could not be questioned that the position of empress had fascinating attraction for her active mind and courageous spirit. But she dearly loved her brother, and her predominant feeling at the moment was regard for his interests. "Albert," she said with great energy, "I will not have you make any sacrifice for me. You will be a good and clever man, and will adorn whatever position you are called to."

"I thank you, Victoria," said the boy gravely. "I am delighted that you think so well of me. But you must not consider I am making a sacrifice. My inclinations are entirely against public life. The position of next heir, and in time of emperor, would give me no pleasure. My ambition—and I am not without it—points to triumphs of a different kind. No success in the council or in the field would give me the gratification that the reception of my paper by the Imperial Institute occasioned me, and the gold medal which I gained without my name as author being known. Why I have dwelt on your fitness for the position, Victoria, is because I do not believe that I should be justified in renouncing the succession unless I could honestly feel that a better person would take my place."

"Albert," interposed the Empress, "let your mother say a word before you proceed further. I will not interfere with any decision that may be arrived at. I leave that to your father, in whose wisdom I have implicit faith. But I must ask you, Have you thought over all contingencies, not only of what has happened in the past or of what is now occurring, but of what the future may have in store?"

"I have, my mother, thought over the future as well as the past."

"You may marry, Albert. Your wife may grieve for the position you have renounced; you may have children: they may inherit your father's grand qualities. Will you yourself not grieve to see them subordinate to their cousins, your sister's children?"

"Mother, I probably shall not marry; and if I do, my renunciation of the succession will justify me in marrying as my heart dictates, and not to satisfy State exigencies. I shall be well assured that whomever I marry will be content to take me for myself, and not for what I might have been. As to the children, they will be educated to the station to which they will belong, surely a sufficiently exalted one."

The Emperor now interposed. "You are young," he said, "to speak of wife and children; but you have spoken with the sense and discretion of mature years. I understand, that if you renounce the succession, you will do so in the full belief that you will be consulting your own happiness and not injuring those who might be your subjects, because you leave to them a good substitute in your sister."

"You have rightly described my sentiments," said the boy.

"Then, Albert," said the Emperor, "I will give my consent to the introduction of a measure that, preserving your rights, will as regards the future give to females an equal right with males to the succession. As regards yourself, I think the Act should give you after your majority a right, entirely depending on your own discretion, of renunciation in favour of your sister, and provide that such renunciation shall be finally operative."

Our history for the present ends with the passage of the Act described by the Emperor; an Act considered to be especially memorable, since it removed the last disability under which the female sex laboured.

IT IS PERHAPS DESIRABLE TO explain that three leading features have been kept in view in the production of the foregoing anticipation of the future.

First, it has been designed to show that a recognised dominance of either sex is unnecessary, and that men and women may take part in the affairs of the world on terms of equality, each member of either sex enjoying the position to which he or she is entitled by reason of his or her qualifications.

The second object is to suggest that the materials are to hand for forming the dominions of Great Britain into a powerful and beneficent empire.

The third purpose is to attract consideration to the question as to whether it is not possible to relieve the misery under which a large portion of mankind languishes on account of extreme poverty and destitution. The writer has a strong conviction that every human being is entitled to a sufficiency of food and clothing and to decent lodging whether or not he or she is willing to or capable of work. He hates the idea of anything approaching to Communism, as it would be fatal to energy and ambition, two of the most ennobling qualities with which human beings are endowed. But there is no reason to fear that ambition would be deadened because the lowest scale of life commenced with sufficiency of sustenance. Experience, on the contrary, shows that the higher the social status the more keen ambition becomes. Aspiration is most numbed in those whose existence is walled round with constant privation. Figures would of course indicate that the cost of the additional provision would be enormous, but the increase is more seeming than real. Every commodity that man uses is obtained by an expenditure of more or less human labour. The extra cost would mean extra employment and profit to vast numbers of people, and the earth itself is capable of an indefinite increase of the products which are necessary to man's use. The additional employment available would in time make work a privilege, not a burden; and the objects of the truest sympathy would be those who would not or who could not work. The theory of forcing a person to labour would be no more recognised than one of forcing a person to listen to music or to view works of art. Of course it will be urged that natives of countries where the earth is prolific are not, as a rule, industrious. But this fact must be viewed in connection with that other fact that to these countries the higher aims which grow in the path of civilisation have not penetrated. An incalculable increase of wealth, position, and authority would accompany an ameliorated condition of the proletariat, so that the scope of ambition would be proportionately enlarged. There would still be much variety of human woe and joy; and though the lowest rung of the ladder would not descend to the present abysmal depth of destitution and degradation, the intensely comprehensive line of the poet would continue as monumental as ever,—

"The meanest hind in misery's sad train still looks beneath him."

A Note About the Author

Sir Julius Vogel (1835–1899) was the eighth Premier of New Zealand and a pioneering science fiction writer. Born in London, he was educated in chemistry and metallurgy at the Royal School of Mines—now part of Imperial College London—before emigrating to Victoria, Australia. There, he worked as an editor for newspapers aimed at the goldmining industry and made a failed run for a seat in Victorian Parliament. In 1861, Vogel moved to Otago, New Zealand, where he founded the *Otago Daily Times* and won an election to the provincial council in 1862. In 1869, having married Mary Clayton two years prior, he retired from provincial government and began serving in the administration of Premier William Fox in various roles. From 1873 to 1875, Vogel served as the first Jewish Premier in New Zealand's history, using his power to expand the nation's railway system, roads, and communication infrastructure. In 1889, following his last stint in parliament, he published *Anno Domini 2000; Or, Woman's Destiny*, the first science fiction novel written by a New Zealander.

A Note from the Publisher

Spanning many genres, from non-fiction essays to literature classics to children's books and lyric poetry, Mint Edition books showcase the master works of our time in a modern new package. The text is freshly typeset, is clean and easy to read, and features a new note about the author in each volume. Many books also include exclusive new introductory material. Every book boasts a striking new cover, which makes it as appropriate for collecting as it is for gift giving. Mint Edition books are only printed when a reader orders them, so natural resources are not wasted. We're proud that our books are never manufactured in excess and exist only in the exact quantity they need to be read and enjoyed.

bookfinity™

Discover more of your favorite classics with Bookfinity™.

- Track your reading with custom book lists.
- Get great book recommendations for your personalized Reader Type.
- Add reviews for your favorite books.
- AND MUCH MORE!

Visit **bookfinity.com** and take the fun Reader Type quiz to get started.

Enjoy our classic and modern companion pairings!